CW00382014

THE MAN WHO
SAW TOO MUCH

CHAPTER ONE

Life after Covid was getting back to normal enough for Parish Councils to be able to meet face to face again.

In the beginning, when Covid first struck and the so called experts were telling us that as we were all going to be dying from it sooner rather than later, councils didn't meet at all, there seemed no point in wasting our final hours having meetings. So we were all locked down en masse.

When that restriction finally eased parish councils were able to meet each other with the aid of a zoom camera set up in the room, which many councillors secretly preferred, as they were able to hold their meetings in the comfort of their own homes, scantily clad if the fancy to dress very casually took them.

That ruling came to an end eventually, and parish councils returned to holding their meetings face to face wherever and whenever they had previously done so. Reluctantly in the case of some participants it had to be said.

I am Mark Montgomery, and at the time when covid first overwhelmed us I was an itinerant clerk with several parishes in my charge, enough to ensure I had a living wage at the end of the month in fact.

Like Edward Orpin who was the Parish Clerk in the 18th Century Bradford on Avon, present day Parish Clerks like me, with several parishes in my care at any given time are highly

skilled and dedicated servants of the Parish
Council they happen to serve.

Three, in fact, in my case.

One of the biggest differences between
Edward Orpin's day and the present times,
however, though many councils might not be
prepared to admit some of the applicants, is that
now the post is truly open to everyone, rather
than the select few. People who come from all
walks of life in fact.

Becoming a Parish Clerk is one of the
most rewarding jobs in a local community I
always thought even before I became one. That
was in fact why I did become one in the end,
because a competent Clerk underpins a good
Council.

The role of Clerk is to ensure that the
Parish Council they work for then, does, as a
whole, conduct its business properly and to
provide independent, objective and professional
advice and to give support whenever the
councillors need it for any reason. And they can
be many and very varied of course.

The Parish councils in the country are
often viewed as the part of government closest
to the people. They are the only local
government tier that represents residents at the
parish level. The Clerk to any Parish Council in
the land, however big or small it happens to be,
is also the Proper Officer of that Council and as
such is under a statutory duty to carry out all
the functions, and in particular to serve or issue

all the notifications required by law of a local authority's Proper Officer in every respect.

The Clerk is also totally responsible for ensuring that the instructions of the Council in connection with its function as a local authority are carried out, being expected to advise the Council on, and assist in the formation of, overall policies to be followed in respect of the Authority's activities and in particular to produce all the information required for making effective decisions and to implement constructively all decisions. Whatever those decisions happen to be.

When you'd been a clerk for as long as I had and served on so many councils in that capacity you have a background knowledge of the job which means you can slip casually into place if changing council as I often have.

Any person appointed to the role of clerk is accountable to the Council for the effective management of all its resources and will report to them as and when required, being the Responsible Financial Officer responsible for all financial records of the Council and the careful administration of its finances.

Specific Responsibilities of a Parish Clerk are to ensure that statutory and other provisions governing or affecting the running of the Council are up to date, observed and reviewed on a regular basis throughout the year.

As well as monitoring and balancing the Council's accounts, clerks have to prepare monthly budget monitoring reports, effectively manage all grants, loans, trustee and savings accounts; regularly reclaim VAT, and pay any National Insurance or other payments to His majesties government, and prepare all records and documents for internal and external audit purposes.

The Parish Clerk also has to ensure that the Council's obligations for Risk Assessment and it's insurance and assets are properly met and annually reviewed as well as preparing, in consultation with appropriate members, of course.

They also have to prepare agendas for meetings of the Council and its Committees, attend meetings, prepare minutes for approval, arrange and attend all meetings of the Council, and its committees and sub-committees. They also have to receive and deal with correspondence on behalf of the Council they serve, sort through it, then take any action required in consequence.

The role is almost always part time working an average of fifteen hours a week depending upon the needs of the Council, so flexibility is required, apart from a very few clerks working for larger local concerns, Attendance at Parish Council meetings is required. Meetings always take place in the evening, in consequence of which the role can be a mix of home and office based activities.

I'd left Mickleton and Stuncott Parish Councils far behind after my experience of first finding one of the councillors dead along a public footpath and then having several attempts made on my own life as a result by the perpetrator of the murder who, not unnaturally I suppose, seeing my survival as a threat to their own continued existence. Not knowing I had no idea at all of their identity and couldn't have given them away even if I'd wanted to do so!

I'd not left being a parish clerk behind, however, because I was currently working for Mooreland Parish Council as well as for Beazley Parish Council, from both of which I'd taken temporary leave of absence when I sat in the hospital bed discussing my life and times and my recent encounters with murder with the man charged with bringing library books around to people unable to get out of their beds to get them themselves.

He was a man I'd seen several times during the short time I'd been in the hospital requiring his services without actually finding out the man's name. Parish Councils varied a great deal in the amount of salary they paid their clerks and the number of hours they were expected to work too.

In my experience though, and that was varied, none of them paid their clerk a reasonable salary anyone was able to live on. Not even the inner city parishes were prepared to do that, many councillors being reluctant to pay their clerk anything above the bare minimum on the grounds it was rate payers money they were handing out in that way and these ratepayers were often the folk they met socially over a drink or two. Something the clerks in my experience very seldom did it had to be said.

In my own case I had up to three parish clerks salaries coming in at any one time, which didn't always allow me to give the attention to each parish I was working for the attention I would have liked to have given them but, being the frugal fellow I was, with no family commitments of any sort, I was able to get by on if I was very careful how I spent the money coming in.

One of the perks of one of the councils I worked for, Beazley Parish Council in fact, in lieu of some part of my salary granted to a previous clerk at some time was free medical treatment at the hospital of my choice as long as it was on their list. A very unusual perk that I was and I was probably the only clerk ever to make use of it.

There had been a period during the early days of covid and the lockdown which had followed it, when hospitals had become no go areas for everyone. Including the nearest and dearest of anyone unfortunate enough to be admitted.

Avery unpopular restriction that one, it had to be said. One which had gradually eased to the extent that folk were able to visit their loved ones in hospital and some were able to have long postponed operations. Though not as many as they'd hoped.

The perk offered by Beazley Parish Council of private medical attention was allowing me to take a few days off from my duties to go into a hospital just over the border in Herefordshire , a place with a football team I had once supported and have what they called a procedure on my knee whatever that meant which would incapacitate me for a few days only. Or so it promised in the brochure of theirs I'd been studying before deciding to go for that one in particular.

Being able to visit a hospital in any way and for any reason had also been put in abeyance for the same misguided reasons parish councils hadn't been able to meet for so long, but those rules and regulations had also been relaxed enough for me to take temporary leave of absence from my roles as clerks to have that minor operation, or procedure, they chose to call it which I'd been waiting for it for a long time and it was what I was doing then.

One of the many benefits of private healthcare is a range of appointment slots designed to suit the individual, and the option to be seen sooner than you would be if relying on the NHS to deal with you and yours.

If you are self-referring, your chosen healthcare provider should provide you with clear instructions of when and where to attend your appointment and what to expect from it.

After your appointment and a diagnosis has been reached, along with a proposed treatment plan, your consultant will update your GP.

9

Your consultant may also recommend a follow up appointment to discuss any test or scan results involved in the consultaion.

At this point, the hospital can give you a fixed or all-inclusive price if it turns out treatment will be needed. The price to include all aspects of the patient's care.

Should you finally choose to go ahead with any treatment, the hospital will arrange your admission. If you're paying for yourself you'll usually pay the initial consultation fee directly to your consultant.

The all-inclusive price will include fees for the consultant, hospital, anaesthetist, follow-up appointment and any outpatient physiotherapy that may be needed. The terms and conditions of payment will be provided.

With private health insurance the insurance company will pay the invoice. However, any excess on the policy must be paid separately.

CHAPTER TWO

St Bartholomew's hospital where I'd chosen to go to have the procedure on my knee carried out was one of the older hospitals in Hereford. Formally one of the main hospitals in the city, it wasn't so anymore.

It was situated near the centre of the city and the staff there had done sterling work when everything was in lockdown due to covid, but since the needs created by the pandemic had passed it had been taken over by a private concern who administered it for the benefit of private industry to use instead, not as part of the national health set up anymore as it had been before.

Despite that it seemed very similar to National Health hospitals I'd been in in the past, most of the staff employed there being former national health workers now paid by the private health industry instead. The nurses wore different uniforms mostly, but the man who'd brought library books round for the benefit of folk unable to leave their beds for whatever reason to choose from, was dressed similarly to them.

I was one of those unfortunates unable to leave my bed for a day or to after having my knee worked on so had to choose from amongst the ones being offered to me to by the man coming round the wards for that purpose. He was wheeling a trolley ahead of him on which the books on offer were displayed for patients

to study at leisure and then to choose a
selection from. Those patients who could leave
their beds to sample his wares did so, those
who couldn't didn't.

Being unable to leave my bed at that time,
because of the procedure which had been
carried ou on my knee, the library man,
knowing I was unable to do otherwise than sit
there and listen to whatever story he chose to
tell me, struck up a desultory conversation with
me whilst I was sorting through those books he
had on offer, looking for one with which I
might be able to pass some of the long hours I
had to spend in my bed, even if it wasn't one I
might normally enjoy reading.

I don't know why I started telling him about
the body I'd found whilst walking in the woods
near the village where I lived, except that the
event had happened recently enough to still be
right in the forefront of my mind.

It hadn't been my only involvement with
murder, as it happened. Chief Inspector
Macdonald had seen to that by the way he took
control of my life when I got involved with him
and manipulated it to his own advantage.
Someone had tried to kill me then too, but only
as an afterthought really when the woman I'd
been on love with at the time had been
deliberately shot by one of his specials in the
hope it would stir up her lesbian lover into
positive action.

The people involved in that hadn't made it
seem as personal as the Black Widow had done

with her attempts on my life though. Attempts on my life, which I'd survived, of course, or I wouldn't have been there to tell the man the story.

At the time I was speaking of I had recently been taken on to be Clerk to Mickleton and Stuncott Parish Council in Shropshire, and the man I'd come upon lying in a crumpled heap in front of a cottage at the side of a long distance path I'd been following at the time, was Benny Bartlett, a councilor on the same parish council as I worked for.

A man I hazarded to be somewhere in his late seventies, or maybe, perhaps, even in his eighties, with an indeterminate accent which might have originated from absolutely anywhere.

Local to the part of Shropshire I lived in on the borders close to Wales, or Welsh itself maybe, though a dialect I hadn't come across anywhere else, if it was.

Rumour said he had once been part of Britain's security services in some capacity or other. Rumours he might easily have made up himself to make his past seem a more colourful to the casual observer.

Rumour didn't also say how he'd been fool enough to allow himself to be inveigled into becoming the only male member of the village's parish council too, by Monica Nesbitt, the formidable lady who was Chair of the Parish Council we both worked for at the time.

Me for a mere pittance of pay for my efforts and him for love I assumed.

Benny Bartlett was a smoker, and though I'd never taken up the habit myself, I'd sometimes join him when he went outside for a fag during meetings, because no one was allowed to smoke in public buildings like the village hall where meetings took place, and I preferred not to be left there without him to deflect Monica's interest from me, as the only male left in the room without him there.

Despite me being a hired hand not a volunteer, I was nevertheless one of that rare breed on Stuncott Parish Council, a man. That being the case Monica Nesbitt spent a lot of time drumming up volunteers amongst the men to serve on her sub committees. So we spent a lot of the time outside the hall moaning about our misfortune in meeting her.

After meetings we'd sometimes go off to a pub to drown our sorrows, spending many an hour there cursing our misfortune in meeting Monica, and our weakness in letting her get away with browbeating us into helping her. Looking for ways out of the web of enforced public spirited activity she'd dragged us into, whilst knowing there wasn't going to be a way out until we'd completed whatever it was she'd set the pair of us doing on that occasion of course.

Finding a body like that led to a lot of repercussions of all sorts in my life at that time, not the least of which were the several attempts made on my own life as a result of it happening to me.

Recalling how close I'd come to dying as a result of some of them without ever knowing who the perpetrator, or perpetrators were, I finished my account to the library book man with the air of someone to whom that sort of thing happened all the time.

I could see him trolling through his own mind in search of something similar which had happened to him at some time to say in response which would trump the tale I'd told him and then some.

He was bound to respond in a similar vein. What man wouldn't have done so? Certainly not the man who brought the library books round. It led to him me telling a reciprocal story of his own about another patient in that hospital but in a different ward, two patients in that hospital I was in in fact, who'd died after borrowing one of his books, despite there not being anything apparently wrong with either of them which could have led to these unexpected deaths.

"Must be a lot of folk who die under those circumstances," I pointed out to him as he finished his story. "It is a hospital after all." I added quite reasonably as it seemed to me.

"Not as many as you'd expect." He contradicted my observation with a frown. "Certainly not unexpected ones. In fact those two men are the only ones who have died here since I took over the role from my predecessor last year."

He paused in his tale, looking into the far distance with a retrospective shake of his head as he replied. "And there was something strange about both those deaths in my opinion....." His voice tailed off into total silence.

"Strange in what way?" I prompted, as he continued to look into the far distance as if seeing something there I couldn't.

"They weren't what you...." He began to explain what he'd meant then, his voice tailed off again, as he seemed to be looking beyond him at something he could see and I couldn't.

"I've said too much this time I think!" He interrupted himself, still looking beyond me as if seeing that someone standing behind me I couldn't, with sudden concern.

"Finish your story." I chided when he didn't continue, turning my head as quickly as I could in that direction, but unable to see anyone there where he seemed to be looking, not easy as to achieve from a sitting position on my bed, as it involved turning my body to look which I couldn't do quickly.

"I've already said too much!" he gathered up the books he'd spread on my bed as if intending to stay at my bedside forever, before hurrying off without a backward glance or another word.

I had expected him to become a bit of a bore on the subject of unexplained murders but

16

just the opposite turned out to be the case. Wanting to exchange my book for another one the next day, the man who'd brought them around didn't appear I enquired why and was told the man had died.

"Died!" I exclaimed in surprise. Blinking a bit at being the recipient of that surprising information.

"It's not that unusual, people do die in hospitals you know?" The ward orderly who'd told me said tetchily.

"Yeah, but not usually the guy doing the library run surely?" I countered suspiciously, still taking in the bombshell he'd exploded under me without apparently realising it. "How did he die anyway?" I wanted to know.

"He fell down the stairs," the orderly said in a matter of fact way as if it was a common occurrence in his world. Though it had to be said I couldn't see how it could be in anyone's world.

"Fell down the stairs!" I repeated in amazement because it certainly wasn't that common in my world, despite my previous experience of working with Chief Inspector Macdonald when life seemed to be very cheap. "And that killed him?" I questioned further in surprise.

"It a long way from the top floor landing, where he began his descent, to the basement, which it where he ended up. The fall would kill anyone," the ward orderly sounded almost gleeful as he said it, "it would kill anyone. You

included I should imagine!" He concluded,
looking me up and down appraisingly as he did
so

CHAPTER THREE

The woman in the black uniform worn by senior nurses at that hospital who I thought might be a sister or something, looked at me in the disbelief that I should be there addressing her at all, having bearded her, if that was the right word to use when dealing with a woman, in her den, and then had spoken to her in a way she probably found lacking in respect for her position in the hospital, whatever that was.

Wanting to find out more about the fate of the man who'd brought round a selection books for people who couldn't get out of their beds for whatever reason, to choose from and who had brought a selection of books to me the day before and then had disappeared without trace, I'd got up early and gone deliberately to the desk where I noticed that the nurses seemed to hang out and chat to each other but there was no one at it at that moment.

I looked into the office which lay behind it and which had some sort of office title emblazoned on the front of it but was devoid of occupants at that time, then stepped cautiously into the room to address the nurse I'd seen in there. A woman dressed entirely in black.

"I was looking for the man who brings a selection of library books round every day to patients who are unable to get out of their beds themselves to choose from." I said.

"Why" She asked sharply, glaring at me as she did so.

"Why am I looking for him?" I asked as the nurse in black continued to glare at me fiercely.

"Yes," I answered her question after a pause to regroup myself and decide on my answer.

"Because it isn't usual for patients to get involved like that in things which don't really concern them." She replied.

"You think not?" I questioned her take on things.

"I think not." She replied. "So why are you asking me about this man and expecting me to have a suitable reply on hand?"

"Because he told me there were two men he knew of who'd died in this hospital without good cause since he'd been coming here handing out books for patients to read?" I replied simply.

"Because he told you there were two men he knew of who'd died in this hospital without good cause since he'd been coming here handing out books for patients to read?" She repeated to me what I'd just told her, in tones of complete and utter disbelief.

"He did, sister." I assumed in my reply that that must be the rank of the woman I was facing, well aware that my words weren't being well received by her.

I could hardly be surprised that they weren't because, even if not true she would have still seen it as a slur on her hospital. Not surprising under the circumstances. "What were the names of these two men who died in our hospital though they shouldn't have done according to you?" She glared back at me, asking what, under the circumstances probably seemed a very pertinent question to her.

Pertinent to me also I had to admit silently to myself without giving that fact away in my reply because I wasn't able to. "He didn't tell me that I'm afraid," our conversation not having progressed that far at the time, I thought, but didn't say so, of disclosing the names of his alleged murder victims to me.

"When were they actually here as patients?" The nurse in black asked another leading question of me. One I couldn't answer as it happened, because my thinking it over hadn't got to that point at the time.

"He didn't tell me that either." I had to concede reluctantly. Very reluctantly it had to be said. Because he hadn't, our conversation not having progressed that far, and now never would, of course.

"Didn't tell you, Mr Montgomery!" The nurse swelled visibly at that in complete disbelief, probably that I should have set this thing in motion without knowing that, at least.

"And then he died immediately afterwards in what seemed very suspicious circumstances to me." I pointed out pertinently. "Falling down several flights of stairs after being pushed by some interested party to start him on his way perhaps!"

My previous experience with murders and murderers making my mind turn to that line of thought more quickly than it might otherwise have done with most patients she'd had to encounter, probably.

"What did they have wrong with the that they shouldn't have died of?" The nurse in black asked me what to her must have seemed an obvious question to be asking at that point, I guess.

"He didn't tell me that either." I had to admit reluctantly again, because he hadn't, our conversation not having progressed that far at the time. And now never would of course, given the circumstances, I thought pertinently again.

"Do you think he might have just been trying to compete with the story you'd just told him," the nurse in the black uniform, who may or may not have been the sister at that hospital, asked what also probably seemed an obvious question to her. "In my experience of men they do that sort of thing a great deal don't they? Trying to be top dog in all walks of life."

"Do they?" I genuinely had no idea at all where the woman was going with that line of thought. "What sort of things do you mean?"

"Compete with each other over inconsequential things." She said simply. Speaking as if to a mentally retarded patient. Looking me up and as appraisingly as she said it as the as the ward orderly before had done. It's the alpha male syndrome taken to extremes. Why did he tell you about this supposed patient in the first place?"

"I'd just told him how someone had tried to kill me when they thought I'd seen them murdering someone else. Even though I hadn't really."

"And he wanted to be the one to slash highest up the wall than you had?" She declared with venom.

"Is that what you mean by that?" I suddenly grasped what she'd been leading towards with her questioning and didn't like the line she was taking at all.

"Something like that, Mr Montgomery, something like that." She agreed with me with a smile I found irritating in the extreme, though I tried to hide the fact. Probably not very successfully I have to say.

"So you won't investigate the story he told me then?" I got straight to the point she'd been trying to make to me without preamble.

"I've got too many other things to do!" She told me caustically. "More important things by far! I haven't time to waste time over something which more than likely didn't happen in the first place!"

"I should think you'll get on better with your investigation, if you intend carrying on with it, once you get back home amongst familiar people and things." Another nurse had joined the other one now, this one not in black though, but in the normal uniform most nurses were wearing. She stood close to the first one as if to express solidarity with her in the face of a stroppy patient, namely me.

"What do you mean I can carry on my investigation at home? You're saying I'm going home then?" I was news to me if I was. As far as I'd noticed no one had got out of the place so swiftly before. In fact most folk seemed to be held back in the place long after they wanted to be free of it and couldn't wait to get away.

"You're going home." The lower echelon nurse confirmed what the one I took to be her superior had said. "I've just been clearing your bed of your belongings in readiness for that to happen!"

"But I'm not going home until the doctor tells me I'm being discharged and he didn't do that when he did his round this morning I promise you. Didn't even look at me as far as I recall!"

"You're going home." The lower echelon nurse confirmed. "You'll find your bed has been cleared to make way for a new patient."

"Yes, you're leaving us, I've been told." The woman in black had returned to confirm the fact. "And that's why your clothes have been moved off your bed in readiness for that to happen."

"I don't think so." I disagreed with that summing up of things. Deciding to stand up for my rights as a patient, as I saw it. "I'm not due to go until the consultant declares me fit. I'm not allowed to leave until the consultant I saw declares me fit enough to do so. It says so in your manifesto! You should read it some time."

"That's all gone by the board I'm afraid." The nurse in black, a tall woman, deliberately moved closer to tower over me threateningly, as she told me authoritatively. "We need your bed for someone else."

"Who?" I enquired sharply. Not believing that story for a moment. Suspecting something more sinister than my bed being needed for another patient was behind my unheralded departure.

"For am an emergency who has just been brought in." The nurse in black, still towering above me, said sharply.

"Where am I supposed to go to." I suddenly felt overwhelmed by events unfolding around me and the certainty they were all stemming from the man seen something her shouldn't before falling down the stairs to his death. "The rest room?"

"Actually you're going home." The nurse in black told me authoritatively as the two nurses joined forces in order to present a united front against me, as an extremely stroppy patient, growing stroppier by the moment it had to be said in the face of such unacceptable treatment.

"Going home?" That was completely unheard of in my brief experience of the hospital. For anyone to be shunted out early like that. Why was it now happening to me at the hands of this seemingly all powerful nurse?

"Yes there's a taxi outside waiting to take you, Mr Montgomery." She refuted my belief it couldn't happen like that despite everything. " The ward Sister has arranged it all for you to happen."

"Take me where?" I demanded unhappily. "There isn't anyone at home to see me in and settle me down." And there wasn't. I didn't live in that kind of environment anymore. Not since my relationship had ended.

"That's your problem." The nurse in black said matter of factly, as the other stood behind her ready to support the other in dealing with me together if I became stroppier than I already was in the face of this unacceptable treatment.

"What am I supposed to do there?" I asked plaintively. Hoping they might reconsider, or tell me they'd just been joking with me. "I'm all on my own there with no one to look after me."

"We've arranged for the district nurse to visit you and settle you into your home." The nurse in black told me. "We thought you'd be pleased to be back there amongst your own things." Even she didn't sound as if she meant it.

"Well I'm not!" I told her sharply. And I wasn't, not happy at all about the treatment I was getting.

"Tough luck." The other nurse took a hand in proceedings. Not sounding for a minute as if she really meant it. "You shouldn't make waves like you've been making if you don't like what happens to you as a result." She pointed out.

"Making waves?" I questioned sharply. Not really having the vaguest idea what she meant by that.

"Making waves." She agreed equally sharply. Not enlightening me what they meant by that at all.

"Asking too many pertinent questions you mean?" I dotted the is and crossed the ts for the women to show I knew why what had just happened to me had happened. "Ones you haven't got an answer for."

"If you want to describe your attempted muck raking in those terms its up to you." The nurse in black told me coldly.

"Muck raking!" I exclaimed in disgust to hear was I saw as legitimate questioning being referred to in that damning way. "Is that what you people call it in this neck of the woods?"

"Muck raking." The other nurse agreed with her superior. "Goodbye Mr Montgomery. And if you get into difficulties at home don't call us, Mr Montgomery, because we certainly won't be answering your call!"

CHAPTER FOUR

Pancho Gomez smiled at me expansively across the expanse of his desk in Carmarthen Police Station. Looking directly into the zoom camera as he did so, not trying to ignore its presence as many people did in my experience. It's good to see you Mark!" He said as if he meant it.

Why he should think so I wasn't sure at that moment it had to be said "Is it? Is it really?" I responded thoughtfully, afraid he might just have been being polite with me for old time's sake.

"Of course." He replied as if the thought had never crossed his mind, though I couldn't see why that would be the case. "Why wouldn't it be?" His eyes met mine as we looked at each other through the medium of that zoom camera we were both using as if borne to it though I, at least found them difficult and unwieldy.

"Because I haven't been in touch with you since the cases involving the murders of Edward Holmes and Benny Bartlett and the attempt on my life by Magda Trofimovitch, the Black Widow, were wound up." I pointed out. Very truthfully in my opinion it had to be said "Now I get in touch with you without warning to ask if you will help for help with another case of murder."

"But that's what friends do isn't it," the inspector retorted expansively, still smiling at me all the while as he did so, "they get in touch with each other at any times of need which occur."

"Is that what we are though Pancho," I answered his question with another question of my own, "friends? Would you say in all honesty that that is what we are? Old friends getting in touch with each other at times of need?"

"I would definitely have described us that way Mark." He replied expansively again. "So what help do you want from me now? And remember that last time it was me taking advantage of you. Not you taking advantage of me. Which reminds me, did you ever get together with that girl, what was her name - Sarah Evans wasn't it I seem to remember? - a special constable wasn't she if I recall?" he interrupted himself at that point with this interpolation of his, "I mean really get together with her?"

"No." I shuddered at the memory he'd awoken for me. "There was never any chance that we would. We weren't each others type at all I always thought, as far as I recall. And I try not to do that too often in relation to her!"

"What became of her anyway?" He asked interestedly. "Even if you didn't keep in touch with her at all. You seemed to be practically living in each others pockets at that time, as I recall."

"Last I heard she was living with that tame policeman who used to follow her around, despite her telling me they weren't an item at all. I always thought that they had more in common with each other than her and me ever did!" I finished my summing up of the relationship sadly.

My getting back in touch with Pancho Gomez by means of Zoom seemed, so far anyway, to have gone along more easily than I'd feared when I'd first contemplated making the move to do so.

I had had experience of zoom meetings when parish councils had been unable to meet face to face when lockdown was coming to an end, and had used them as an interim alternative, not that I was altogether taken with using them, much preferring the encounters in the flesh were used to be familiar with before covid changed everything.

I'd hoped the police would have got used to using them too. An approach like the one I'd just made seemed the only way forward for me after being so ignominiously expelled from the hospital the way I had been by the two nurses. So I'd done just that, and considering my options in regard to my next course of action, had got in touch with Pancho Gomez a police inspector usually based at Carmarthen police station, but who I'd previously met when he'd been on loan to Shrewsbury police force as a temporary measure. Helping to solve a murder I'd become involved with.

Making a tentative approach to him via zoom he'd accepted more welcomingly than I'd feared he might. I could have got in touch with

Chief Inspector Macdonald. I suppose, but as I'd told him at our final meeting that there was no way I would ever work with him again after the way he'd manipulated me before, and that I'd rather become a parish clerk than ever work with him again, I felt I'd get in touch with Inspector Gomez instead.

He mulled over what I'd said to him in my opening foray which was aimed at getting what was and what wasn't out of the way before asking what it was I was wanting from him in the way of help.

"I found myself rather shunted out of the hospital without warning," I replied, still feeling embittered at the memory of my treatment, "and without being able to investigate in any way the death of the man who brought the library books round, a man whose name I still don't know. Whether he fell down those stairs accidently or was helped on his way by someone pushing him to his death down the stairs without any warning I also still don't know. And that was after he told me there were two men he knew of who'd been patients in the hospital and who'd died without good cause"

"He told you there were two men he knew of who'd been patients in the hospital for a while before dying without good cause did he?" He picked up on what I'd just said and asked it back again as an opening gambit.

"He did." I agreed with his summing up of things as I had reported them, which seemed to have been more readily accepted by him than it had been by the two nurses in the hospital before him.

"And what were the names of these two men?" He enquired thoughtfully. Smiling into the camera again as he did so. Waiting for a response from me that I couldn't give him unfortunately.

"He didn't tell me that I'm afraid." I had to admit, realising in that moment that I didn't really know much about what he'd said.

Certainly not enough to be tilting at windmills the way I was. It was only because the man had died so suddenly afterwards and I'd been ejected so summarily from the hospital afterwards, and taken against the nurse in black in a big way as a result, and then had had nothing to occupy my mind at home after being sent there so ignominiously it seemed to me, that it had seemed I had to take the matter further the first chance I got. If none of those things had happened in the order they had, I might not have.

Getting in touch with the police after that had seemed the most obvious course of action open to me to take as a result, and so I had done just that. His next question seemed to indicate that the inspector was thinking that himself.

"When were they actually there as patients, these two men who died?" He persevered asking the sort of question only someone intending to investigate the matter further would be likely to be asking, but not one I could answer unfortunately.

"He didn't tell me that either, I'm afraid." I said sadly becoming increasingly aware that my answers were not likely to make anyone other than me investigate the matter further. The two nurses who had thrown me out the way they had were what had made me carry things through to their conclusion and the unexplained death of the library man not to be allowed to just disappear into the ether.

"What did they have wrong with the that they shouldn't have died of?" Inspector Gomez, probably wishing by then that he'd never answered my call, persevered in the face of my ineptitude.

"He didn't tell me that either." I had to admit, wonderingly, If I was going to expect other people to continue the matter on my behalf, I needed to find out the answer to leading questions like that.

"Do you think he might have just been trying to compete with the story you'd just told him?" He asked a question very similar to what one of the nurses had asked me. "You did say you began by telling him what had gone down when the black widow tried to kill you didn't you, Mark? You might even have been a bit of a celebrity to him after telling him your story about the Black Widow trying to kill you. I suppose you did do that didn't you? That might have made him try to better your story with one of his own mightn't it? You did tell him that story I suppose?" He was looked intently into his zoom lense as he was asking me the question.

"You think he saw me as some sort of celebrity as a result of that?" I feigned ignorance of the question which had been put to me before. "I didn't feel at the time that he was doing that."

"Whether you thought he was or not, he still might have been trying to outdo your story with one of his own mightened he Mark." He dotted the is and crossed the ts for me in case I hadn't grasped them myself.

"I didn't get the feeling he was doing that and the way I was shunted out of that hospital so quickly once I'd started asking questions suggested to me someone was getting cold feet about my investigation. And getting me out of their hair as quickly as it was possible for them to do!"

"Someone with something to hide do you think?" The Inspector asked reflectively as he stared interrogatively into the camera on his police issue computer.

"Someone with something to hide." I agreed as I stared equally reflectively into the camera of mine too.

"I'll have to look into what you've just told me and get back to you as soon as I can," he promised with a smile.

"You were on secondment to Shrewsbury when I met you before." I pointed out to him thoughtfully. "Are you able to investigate a crime this far outside your patch?" I asked him as a disquieting thought occurred to me.

"Leave it to me," had the thought occurred to him before I suggested it I don't know. "I'll make a few enquiries and get back to you either way." He promised as if he meant it and why shouldn't he, unless he had a lot else on his plate of course, and the Pancho Gomez I was meeting now was one who promised rather than delivered.

"Via Zoom again?" I suggested as he said it. "We'll have to make an appointment which each other if we decide to dot that" "How would three o'clock tomorrow afternoon suit you?" He asked after a bit of thought on the subject.

"Three o'clock tomorrow afternoon suits me fine." I fell in easily with the suggestion as he'd made it.

CHAPTER FIVE

One of the parish councils I was clerk to had to have a meeting before then though and it was after a that particular meeting that one of the councillors, a middle aged women approached me.

After having ejected from the hospital so summarily the way I was, I had decided to get back real life more quickly than I might otherwise have done by returning to attending parish council meetings which had gone back to face to face meetings as a general rule instead of meeting by Zoom.

I felt that if I didn't move about any more than I had to during the course of a meeting, or whilst I was preparing for it beforehand, my processed knee ought to be able to stand any strain it was subjected to as a result.

Beazley Parish Council, the council due to meet, had a complement of five, with two vacancies at that moment.

Of those five three were women. The men were both farmers working their own land and intending to get back to real life after the meeting as swiftly as they could. One of the women members was a lady who had taken early retirement and saw serving on the parish council as a means of putting something back into the community in which she lived.

Two of the other women councillors on Beazley Parish Council helped their husbands run rental properties. Mostly barn conversions of one sort or another and they could be very varied.

It was one of those two women who spoke to me after the meeting as I was collecting up my papers to put into my briefcase and go home. A lady whose name as I recalled it from previous parish council meetings I'd attended before the lockdown, was Alexandra Merrydew.

"I hear on the grapevine that you're interested in finding out about two men who died under circumstances you believe to be suspicious, whilst they were patients at the hospital you've just been being treated in," she said, looking at me speculatively across the tops of her spectacles.

I put down my brief case, which I'd just picked up in readiness to go home. Refraining from asking who it was had told her that I was doing that. "I am that." I agreed with her assessment of things.

"My daughter worked there as a nurse in that hospital you were in for a while, St Bartholomew's hospital wasn't it, though she now works elsewhere in the health industry. I was wondering what it was you wanted to know so I could ask her, and report back to you during our next meeting. If that would be of any help to you of course, she paused to await my response."

"Actually it's a long time to wait until the next meeting" I pointed out after a bit of thought on the subject, "do you think you could text your daughter now and get her answers now," I said hopefully, "rather than me have to wait until the next meeting, which isn't going to be for another couple of months." By which time you might have forgotten that you ever made the offer, I thought to myself.

"You mean you want me to get in touch with my daughter now, do you?" She smiled at me brightly.

"If you wouldn't mind doing me that little favour." I said, hopeful that by this means I ought to find out more about the unexplained deaths from her daughter who no longer worked at the hospital, than from nurses who still did.

"How did you come to be in there anyway as a private patient?" She asked the leading question other councillors would probably have liked to ask if they'd been given the opportunity to do so. "We weren't paying for it here at Beazley Parish Council were we, I hope?" she asked me sharply

"No, of course not," I said quickly, feeling it was no business of hers who had paid for it, even if it was actually her and her fellow villagers who had paid for it. "Stuncott Parish Council were the ones who were paying." I lied through my teeth with a knowing smile, accompanied by a wink.

"The one the councillor you found dead in the woods worked for?" She asked, more knowledgeably than I had expected anyone on that council to be.

"Yes." I replied, wondering exactly how it was she'd come to enjoy that snippet of information about me.

"How did you come to have private treatment anyway?" She demanded of me. "I always thought it was a bit of a rip-off when people chose it over the NHS. Especially with my daughter being in the business!"

"Going private with your healthcare is a real investment, and one which is becoming more common in the UK." I explained with what I hoped was a winning smile, but which was probably nothing of the sort under the circumstances and wouldn't prevent her looking into the matter further, which was the outcome I was hoping for.

"You may choose to invest in private healthcare for a range of reasons, including a need or desire to be seen as soon as possible. In fact, analysis of data from the Private Healthcare Information Network has found that there were sixty nine thousand self-funded treatments in the United Kingdom in the final three months of 2021. A thirty nine percent rise on the same period before the pandemic struck us all so fiercely.

Most patients can get private treatment after a referral from their NHS GP. Alternatively, you can opt to pay for a private GP consultation to be seen earlier.

Private hospitals or clinics may see patients without a referral; however, they may need to consult with your GP before providing treatment.

However, you may not need a GP referral if you would like to book a diagnostic scan or physiotherapy. Typically, if you have been referred by a GP, they will recommend a suitable consultant for you. They will write a referral letter on your behalf......"

"I suppose most private healthcare providers host a directory of consultants which you can search though by location and speciality?" She asked.

"Yes," I agreed. "At this stage, if you have private medical insurance, as I did courtesy of Stuncott Parish Council," I continued to lie though my teeth, "in that case you will need to check that the consultant is covered by your policy.

You will also need to get an authorisation reference from your insurer. If you're unsure, you can contact your insurer to check. One of the many benefits of private healthcare is a range of appointment slots to suit you, and the option to be seen sooner.

Just like Stuncott Parish Council did on my behalf," I lied again, because it had actually been her and her fellow councillors had paid the procedure on my behalf. "If you have private medical insurance, your insurance company can make an appointment with the consultant on your behalf.

If you are self-referring, you can call the private healthcare provider directly to make an appointment with a specific consultant. The tests and scans, I needed were booked in before my initial consultation. My chosen healthcare provider providing me with clear instructions of when and where to attend your appointment and what to expect from it.

That was my opportunity to ask as many questions as I needed to, so I could go away feeling well-informed and with a treatment plan. As I was paying for myself I paid the initial consultation fee directly to my consultant. The all-inclusive price included fees for the consultant, hospital, anaesthetist, follow-up appointment and any outpatient physiotherapy that may be needed. With private health insurance the insurance company will pay the invoice. However, any excess on the policy must be paid separately.

"In my case it was being paid for by Stuncott Parish Council, so the matter didn't arise at all. Now, weren't you about to text your daughter a question or two before we both set off to our respective homes?"

I gave her a gentle reminder of her promise. She responded to my prompt by reaching into her bag, fetching a mobile phone out of it, and doing a bit of rapid texting on it, whilst I looked on and explained about how I came to have health insurance in the first place.

"Did she tell you anything?" I asked, having watched impatiently as she tapped and read, tapped and read, then tapped and read again.

"She said there were two men who died after operations which went wrong," she told me as, task completed, she read again to herself what her daughter had texted her.

"She didn't tell you their names I suppose?" I asked impatiently as she seemed to have taken an inordinate amount of time over this contact with her distant daughter.

"Annie said that one of men who died was cremated the other one was buried." She said at last. "So there'll be no remains of the first one for the police to investigate of course."

"You don't know where I suppose?" I asked impatiently again, feeling that all this texting between phones was taking a very long time.

"I do actually" Alexandra told me, as she reread again what her daughter had sent her, and then came back with the name of a nearby village and with Edward Evans and Christopher Mayhew as the men's names.

"Evans was the one who was buried Mayhew the one who was cremated, he died first." She told me. Having read it all through again.

"We'll need to get Mr Mayhew exhumed if they'll do I then." I said thoughtfully, wondering how easy that was going to be to achieve.

The same difficulty had occured to her it seemed. "I don't imagine it will be an easy thing to set up." She said with a frown.

"No." I agreed with a similar frown to hers I'm sure. "See you at the next meeting."

"See you at the next meeting." She agreed, and we made our separate ways home from the parish council meeting.

CHAPTER SIX

"Remind me what a parish clerk actually does," Pancho Gonzales suggested as we faced each other via the zoom camera at the hour of the day we'd agreed on, on the day we had agreed on too. "I expect you told me when you helped me before but if you did I've forgotten.

"Becoming a Parish Clerk is one of the most rewarding jobs in a local community," I replied, because a competent Clerk underpins a good Council. "The role of Clerk is to ensure that the Council as a whole conducts its business properly and to provide independent, objective and professional advice and support to the councillors you work with.

Being a Clerk puts you in the centre of things, but only if you carry out the duties properly, of course. The County Council, on the other hand, is responsible for strategic services such as highways, education, libraries, social services, strategic planning and refuse disposal.

The Parish councils in the county are often viewed as the part of government closest to the people. And they are the only local government tier that represents residents at the parish level, of course. The Clerk to the Council will be the Proper Officer of the Council and as such is under a statutory duty to carry out all the functions, and in particular to serve or issue all the notifications required by law of a local authority's Proper Officer.

The Clerk will be totally responsible for ensuring that the instructions of the Council in connection with its function as a local authority are carried out properly and to the best of the clerk's abilities.

The Clerk is expected to advise the Council on, and assist in the formation of, overall policies to be followed in respect of the Authority's activities and in particular to produce all the information required for making effective decisions and to implement constructively all decisions.

They also have to attend all the meetings that have been called and prepare minutes for approval afterwards, arrange and attend all meetings of the Council and all meetings of its committees and sub-committees, receive correspondence and documents on behalf of the Council and deal with the correspondence or documents or bring such items to the attention of the Council.

On top of that they also have to issue correspondence as a result of instructions concerning the known policy of the Council, including lodging all representations made by the Council as statutory consultee on planning applications within the time frame given by the Local Planning Authority.

All Parish Council meetings are open to the public. They are led by the Council's Chairman, or by their deputy if the chair is unable to attend for some reason, and advised by the Parish Clerk who is there to see that business is conducted properly, and within the law of the land.

The Clerk to the Council will be the Proper Officer of the Council and as such is under a statutory duty to carry out all the functions, and in particular to serve or issue all the notifications required by law of a Local Authority's Proper Officer.

The Parish Clerk will be totally responsible for ensuring that the instructions of the Council in connection with its function as a Local Authority are carried out by the appropriate person.

The Clerk is expected to advise the Council on, and assist in the formation of, overall policies to be followed in respect of the Authority's activities and in particular to produce all the information required for making effective decisions and to implement constructively all decisions.

The person appointed will be accountable to the Council for the effective management of all its resources and will report to them as and when required. The Clerk is the Responsible Financial Officer and responsible for all financial records of the Council and the careful administration of its finances, in order to do that properly they have to attend all meetings of the Council and all meetings of its committees and sub-committees too.

They also have to receive correspondence and documents on behalf of the Council and deal with the correspondence or documents or bring such items to the attention of the Council as well as issuing correspondence as a result of instructions of, or the known policy of the Council.

On top of that they have to receive and report on invoices for goods and services to be paid for by the Council and to ensure such accounts are met, as well as issuing invoices on behalf of the Council for goods and services and ensuring payment is received, as well as monitoring the implemented policies of the Council to ensure they are achieving the desired result and, where appropriate, suggest modifications.

Being a Clerk to a Parish or Town Council is a job not a spare time activity, as some people try to see it, I'm afraid. Councils operate nationally recognised rates of pay and conditions. There is a clear job description, a contract of employment and pay in accordance with national rates for the size of council.

Skills and attributes needed include a good deal of common sense, confidence to handle the administrative work, being a good organiser, being IT literate and able to get on with most people. Underwriting these qualities is a sense of public duty - of wanting to help others in the community. The job is no different whether its clerk to a large council or clerk to a small councils.

What is different however, is the amount of time needed to deal with the volume of business.

For small parishes, what might be needed is only a few hours each week, while for the larger councils it could be a full-time commitment and for some very busy parishes, there might be work enough for a full-time clerk and a part-time assistant clerk.

Most council meetings are held 'out of hours' so being a part-time clerk is not just a daytime activity. Councils operate nationally recognised rates of pay and conditions, clerks should expect a clear job description, a contract of employment and pay in accordance with national rates for the size of council, which will be dependent on the skill levels, experience and qualifications of the clerk in question."

I finished what I'd been saying and looked into the lens of the zoom camera in front of me expectantly, assuming that he'd been paying proper attention all the time I'd been talking but the trouble with zoom meetings was that he might not even have been there to be seen but had been off doing something else and simply reappeared when it was obvious I was requiring an answer to something.

Whether he had been doing any of those things I'd feared he might have been doing, I thought jaundicedly, or had been there all the while I'd been talking but simply been out of sight, Pancho Gonzales looked at me thoughtfully through the lens of his own zoom camera when I'd finished my discourse, seemingly gathering himself before giving his reply as I did so.

"I checked with the hospital authorities as you suggested," he said matter of factly, as his opening gambit of the meeting,"and they said they couldn't find any evidence of men dying in recent times who shouldn't have done so."

"They would say that wouldn't they?" I countered bitterly, glaring into the lens my own camera as I did so. " But how are you going to prove they're lying about that unless you look into the matter more deeply?"

"Perhaps." He agreed non-committally. Smiling in a manner he had intended to be placatingly as he did so. But anything but as far as I was concerned.

"Well I happen to know from a different source" I said sharply, "that the two men were called Evans and Mayhew. Edward Evans was the one who was buried, whilst Christopher Mayhew the one who was cremated, he died first."

"You heard from a different source? He questioned equally sharply. "What different source, and how have you suddenly found it?" He glared into the lens of his own camera as belligerently as I had glared into mine probably.

"What about the man falling down the stairs?" I ignored his question to ask him one of my own equally sharply. "They had to admit to that because it had only just happened to him, but they say it was an accident pure and simple. Something, they said, which could have happened to anyone."

He gave no indication of whether he believed or not what he'd been told by the hospital authorities, probably represented by the nurse in black. "Unless you make yourself particularly unpleasant to someone and say point blank you don't believe them, no one is going to break ranks." I pointed out pertinently into the zoom lense.

"You think I should have a meeting with someone and make it clear I don't believe them?" He picked up on the you're not doing enough to sort this out vibes I hoped I was sending him.

"Yes." I said caustically. Glaring into the camera as if it was the Zooms fault all this was going on, not the nurse in black. "Why not do that?"

"Because I don't know that I don't believe their version rather than yours." He said simply. "There's only the man you don't know the name ofs word for it that any of their records they showed me are suspect after all!"

"The man who was tipped down the stairs to his death before he could reveal all to me." I pointed out sharply, in case he might have forgotten that pertinent fact in the heat of the moment.

"I don't know that there's anything else I could have done about that story he told you, Mark whether its true or false." He declared pertinently.

"You could insist on checking the records." I told him belligerently, pointing out a further course of action he could take on himself if he chose to but, feeling he probably wouldn't do so.

"I could," he agreed easily, "but it wouldn't be easy and how would know if they showed me the right records or not. There's no one you met whilst you were in hospital you could go and visit?" He queried.

"There weren't many." I said fatalistically. "I wasn't in there long enough for that. And they probably wouldn't let me into their homes anyway, giving covid as an excuse for that of course."

"It has a lot to answer for covid." He pointed out sadly, staring into the very lens of his camera as he did so.

"It does." I agreed sadly. "You know, perhaps if I went walking in the woods again like I did before, someone would pop up and do for me the way they did for Benny Bartlett that time!"

"Do you think you're fit enough to go walking like that yet, Mark, when you've only just had as operation haven't you." He asked pertinently.

"You're right of course." I agreed very reluctantly with what he'd said to me, still feeling that was something more I could have done, should have done even.

"What do you think we ought to do now in that case?" He asked again, as he had done before.

"Have another Zoom meeting in a day or two in case anything turns up in the meantime?" I suggested the only course of action as far as I could see.

"Have another Zoom meeting in a day or two." He agreed with my suggestion easily enough. Too easily, I thought, if the truth be known. We signed off into our separate Zoom lenses.

Mine at least going blank immediately afterwards. Perhaps as a result of the doubts about getting involved with me again he was having already.

CHAPTER SEVEN

We didn't have to wait that long, however, because the next evening there was a ring at the doorbell just as I was watching tv. A football match of some sort it was. The FA cup or the World Cup or something. Not anything I was interested in enough to want to carry on watching it though.

When I went to answer the door I found it was Alexandra Merrydew, the councillor who'd helped me out over the unexpected deaths in the hospital I'd been in, and I couldn't help noticing she was carrying a bottle of wine with her.

"Did your daughter tell you something else about the goings on at that hospital I was in you thought you should pass on to me?" I asked, wondering why she'd come round to my house unannounced, if it wasn't for that reason.

"What more was there to tell us after Annie said that one of men who died was cremated the other one was buried." She said at last. "And that Edward Evans was the one who was buried, whilst Christopher Mayhew the one who was cremated, and that he died first." She completed the set of dodgy dealings.

"So the late Christopher Mayhew is the one we want to have exhumed if the authorities will do it." I said, still pondering on the possibilities.

"That's for the future though," she said, brandishing a bottle of something towards me.

"I thought I'd bring round a bottle for us to share."

"Shouldn't it have been me taking you a bottle for services rendered when you helped me out at the council meeting the other night, not round the other way like this with you bringing a bottle of wine to me?" I pointed out to her.

She smiled. Making no response to that remark at all but looking around the room proprietarily. "I can't help noticing that you seem to be on your own in this house," she said at last, "no woman around as far as I can see. Nor any sign of one having been here at all in the recent past either."

"There isn't Alexandra." I agreed with her assessment of my circumstances. Wondering where, if anywhere it was all going to lead us to however.

"That's not because you don't like women, surely?" She probed ingenuously. "You don't prefer men's company to women's do you Mark?"

"Oh I like women well enough," I put her mind at rest on that score if that was the response she was looking for, "I used to have a regular girl friend – not living here of course – she lived, lives, with her father who farms at Stuncott…

"But not living with you?" She interrupted. "That's a relief. I thought I might have summed you up wrongly at the parish council meeting. You never really know these days where it is that people's fancies along those lines are directed."

"Well my preferences are definitely directed towards women, but not towards Sarah Evans anymore, if they ever were towards her. Sarah Evans is definitely not living with me!" I put her mind to rest on that score.

"Why not?" She asked as if she had the right to ask such a question of me, which I suppose as things turned out in the end, she did have that right.

"We didn't ever really hit it off I'm afraid," I thought it through before answering her question, "we only met though me finding that body in the woods …"

"That was the councillor who's body you found after he'd died in mysterious circumstances wasn't it?" She cut in interrogatively at that point.

"If you like to describe it that way." I conceded the point after consideration of what had happened for a minute or two before answering.

"How would you describe them then?" She asked me sharply, as if she was in doubt on some point of order. "Unusual at the very least I'd say."

"So why have you brought the bottle of wine round to my house?" I decided to ignore the question completely as not being worthy of response from me. "To tell you about finding the body in the woods that day?"

"I'd be disappointed if that's all we do his evening." She replied enigmatically, smiling back at me with a very broad smile on her face as she did so.

"Don't you have a husband?" I was fairly certain her name on my list of councillors when I'd checked it, had had a Mrs Something or other in front of it.

"I do." She agreed with my assessment of the situation in which I found her, adding after a pause, "but I'm afraid he's away at the moment."

"Away, but away where though Alexandra?" I asked her what seemed to be a very reasonable follow up question from my point of view I had to say.

Not a reasonable follow question as far as she was concerned though apparently, because it seemed to take an age for her to answer it. "Abroad." She replied shortly.

"So not likely to come back in a hurry then?" I asked her. The likelihood of that happening being of some interest to me it had to be said.

"We drove each other mad when were weren't able to get away from each other during lockdown." She said poignantly. "So now we spend as little time in each others company as we can."

"That's why you came visiting?" I asked what seemed another reasonable follow up question, not knowing the woman in front off me at all well.

"That's why I came visiting." She confirmed with a smile which had a question attached to it. "What were you doing before I came visiting you Mark?"

"Watching the football on the tv." As the set was in front of me turned on and tuned to that station, it seemed a fairly obvious fact to report to her.

"How about you sort out a couple of glasses for us and we sit down and watch the rest of the match together and see where that takes us?" She looked at me questioningly as she said it.

"Are you always as forward as that?" I asked. Looking at her just as questioningly as she was looking at me at that moment I as I asked it. I expect.

"I am when I see someone I've taken a liking to." Alexandra said simply, by way of response to the question Id just asked her.

"And you've taken a liking to me?" I asked her with a disbelieving smile on my face, because that sort of thing didn't usually happen to me where women were concerned unfortunately.

"You could say that." She looked me up and down in a repeat of the proprietary look of before. Sizing me up obviously, but sizing me up for what I wondered as I returned her look with interest. "We'd better not waste that bottle you've brought with you then." I saw my sexual horizons broadening swiftly with one fell stroke.

"Do you think your knee has recovered enough to spend the night in bed with me?" She asked with a pensive smile. Looking at the offending limb with interest as she did so I noticed. I too studied the limb in question once her offer was on the table.

"There's only one way to find that out." I remarked gleefully as, almost battling with each other to be first, we headed for the stairs together. And there was, it was true.

"Lead the way Mark." She was getting to her feet in readiness for what she hoped was going to follow as she said it to me. So I did what she'd suggested and we found ourselves sharing my big double bed for the rest of the night once that bottle of wine was finished. And that took a while.

I sort of heard her leaving my bed in the morning, but she didn't make enough noise to wake me fully nd I was alone by the time I woke properly in the morning, and lay there in my bed contemplating what had befallen me in the night wonderingly.

CHAPTER EIGHT

It was the next day when someone rang a peal of notes on my doorbell, repeating their efforts only moments later it seemed to me, and I opened the door to find Pancho Gomez looking as if he was about to ring the bell a third time, whilst in the background a squad car I took to be the one he'd just driven to my home in fretted iimpatiently in the background.

I was surprised to see him there as he had only contacted me via Zoom since I'd made contact with him over the man who'd fallen down the stairs to his death whilst I was in the hospital.

The first meeting I'd ever had with him had been when I'd found a dead body in Benny Bartlett's cottage and Special Constable Sarah Evans had tried to have me arrested for it, unsuccessfully of course, since I hadn't carried out the murder.

"Why have you murdered Edward Holmes?" The man in the dark suit, who'd come alone and without a squad car in response to Sarah Evans call to the local police station, and I didn't know yet as Pancho Gonzales, asked conversationally, after studying me in silence for a few minutes more and having made no move to relieve me of some papers Id lifted from the dead man to examine more thoroughly at home and was still trying to manoeuvre into a more comfortable position.

Perhaps I'd hidden them well enough to be invisible to him before he was aware of what I'd done. And he thought my movements were caused by no more than an extraneous itch, or a nervous twitch of some sort I was dealing with as privately as I could.

"Are you a part of the group he told me that he had been investigating on behalf of the newspaper he works for, just a day or two ago?" He asked conversationally.

"I've not murdered anyone!" I'd responded fiercely, angry at having the charge thrown at me for a second time in such a short space of time and still completely falsely. "I didn't really know Edward Holmes, other than seeing him around occasionally." I tried not to look at the man lying on the sofa. "Certainly not well enough to do that to him anyway officer."

"No, I think you may be telling the truth about that," the man nodded as if he might be meaning what he said, but went on studying me speculatively nevertheless. "You shouldn't have broken into the cottage the way you did and got yourself apprehended by Special Constable Evans the way you did if you didn't want to be arrested for it though." He went from studying me speculatively for a few more minutes to suddenly offering me an explanation for his presence there.

"I'm with the police by the way." He said. In case I hadn't deduced it for myself. "Inspector Gomez. On attachment to your local force here." He went on in a heavily accented tone of voice.

"Perhaps if you haven't murdered anyone, you are here because of drugs then. Why you have broken into what it is patently obvious to me isn't your cottage, is because of drugs? For the drug smuggling going on in the area. Someone had left you a fix hidden somewhere in the cottage you came here to collect it?" He paused and went back to studying me speculatively whilst he waited for me to admit or deny the charges he'd levelled at me.

"On attachment from where?" I'd asked, rather than answer his question, which I considered to be no more than rhetorical, having never had any dealing of any sort with such things. Picking up on his name, his general appearance, and his accent I went on to ask a question of my own. "Madrid? Barcelona?"

I was wondering what could have been happening in our little village to stir Interpol, if that was who he was with, into taking such an interest in it.

He'd studied the tips of his fingers carefully for a minute or two before looking back at me to deliver his reply. A reply which didn't at first seem to be any sort of response to what I'd just asked him. Just as my reply hadn't been any sort of answer to the question he'd just asked me.

"Perhaps Mr Holmes was killed by one of the two hombres he was investigating for his

61

newspaper I believe," he said, "Henry or Eddie Hardmann. Brothers who work out of Manchester, to run a gang whose activities were tracked over a number of years on the Spanish mainland.

Henry Hardmann until recently was Chairman of your Parish Council here I believe."

"Was he?" I asked in tones which I hoped suggested I had had no involvement whatsoever with the man. Far less be trying to hide papers, which may have been to do with him and his business, down my top more securely than they were.

"He was," the man in the dark suit said, "and even though he and Eddie are brothers, the two hombres, as criminals who don't really trust each other are prone to do, quarreled over the way their enterprise was run, and over the division of spoils, to the extent that they are currently carrying out a turf war for control of their gang on Spanish soil, even though they are English.

Henry has always lived in The Marches and handled this side of things. Eddie has lived in various parts of Spain for a number of years and handled the Spanish side. The brothers, though apparently at war with each other have, as brothers whose private conflict is purely a family affair carried on behind closed doors and no business of anyone else as far as they are concerned, have links to various criminal organizations throughout the world, specifically with South American drug cartels.

Now it seems they may be involved with money laundering on a grand scale. Money which Henry was channeling through your Parish Council amongst other enterprises of his."

"So you are on attachment from the Spanish police?" I interrupted. Interested to find out more about the man who seemed so different from the other police officer who was present namely — Special Constable Sarah Evans.

"From the police in Wales as it happens." He contradicted by assumption. "I'm on attachment from Carmarthen actually," he laughed expansively.

"Carmarthen," I'd repeated, running the name carefully through my mind and testing it with my tonsils, "It's somewhere I don't think I know of."

"Not many people do." He laughed again. "Or not many people know they know it. Its a County town right in the middle of Wales. You've probably driven round it rather than go through it when you've been heading west.

"But your name," I protested, "Your appearance!" I didn't add to the mix, and your indecipherable accent too!"

"Blame my parents for that!" He laughed again. "Or my father anyway. He was a policeman in Spain. My mother came back to Wales, where she'd originated from, when the marriage broke down, and I took up the family trade when I grew up enough to do so. My grandfather had been a policeman in Spain too. So it's really in the blood as far as I'm concerned. Have you got any family connections to what you do?" He asked.

"None I know of." I assured him. "Being Parish Clerk is something to try not to let other people find out about if you're doing it. It's not a career passed down through the generations."

"That's what do you do to earn your crust is it? Parish Clerk." He commented, picking up the remark and running with it. "Tell me about it then." He instructed. "It might have some bearing on what you were doing here with this dead man you say you didn't have anything to do with the killing of."

So, after giving it a few minutes thought, I did as he'd asked, and told him how I had come to discover Benny Bartlett's body outside the ruined cottage in the hills and how that had led in its turn to Monica Nesbitt inveigling me into breaking into the cottage and being apprehended by Inspector Gomez. "All I really want out of life is to be allowed to live a quiet one," I assured the man confronting me unhappily, "not to be whisked away in its merry whirl the way it has done lately."

"So, if you were not involved in smuggling any sort of contraband around the country, or helping anyone else smuggle any contraband around it either, not drugs, nor money, nor any of the other things my colleagues and I are really in pursuit of, in that case then, what are you doing here in this cottage where it seems that you have no business to be?"

"Trying to help a woman in need who'd asked for my help. That was all I was doing." I'd told him bleakly at the time, thinking it through carefully.

"A woman. Joder!" He'd changed to Spanish in order to swear more fluently. Something I was to find was a habit of his, switching from language to language when it suited him, and not just between English and Spanish. "They have taken over the 'world and rule our lives these days it seems to me!"

"Now back in the present. "the Inspector said,

"It was a woman who directed me to you again, Mark my friend, though not to accuse you of committing a crime yourself this time." He paused and looked at me speculatively Seemingly waiting for a response of some sort from me. He got it in spadefuls.

"I don't understand!" I protested and I didn't. Not one iota of what he'd just said to me did I have any sort of understanding of at that moment but that ignorance was about to change.

"Nevertheless it was a friend of yours you may know of, a Mrs Alexandra Merrydew, who I think you may know quite well, very well in fact, with whom you may well have discussed your recent stay in hospital and the man who fell to his death as he was about to give you the name of two folk who died there unexpectedly, shall we say Mark my friend?"

"And?" I glared at the policeman as I would have glared at her if she'd been there to glare at.

"Mrs Merrydew searched me out in my office very early this morning to say that her daughter told her that the nurse you spoke of who had you thrown out of the hospital so unexpectedly…

"The nurse in black!" I interrupted the Inspector fiercely, putting a name to her and wondering why the woman was pursuing me so relentlessly it seemed.

"Well she was not only the wife of one of the men who died, unexpectedly according to your libraryman" Inspector Gomez told me with a grim smile, but having a relationship of the wife of the other man who died unexpectedly."

"Why didn't she tell me this as well as telling you Pancho?" I demanded of him despite the fact he couldn't possibly answer the question of course.

"You'll have to take that up with her Mark!" He said, with an expansive smile grinning at me and winked knowingly as I glared at him in response.

"I will when I see her again!" I promised the grinning policeman with a scowl of my own to counter that smile of his which irritated me more than a little.

"She told me that Evans was the one who was buried Mayhew the one who was cremated, he died first." He chose to ignore the fact he was coming between us big time in all this subterfuge.

"She searched you out to tell you this?" I was always surprised by the deviousness of the women I came in contact with, even though it seemed to happen to me with greater and greater frequency.

"She did." He laughed at the surpise on my face.

"Why didn't she wait for me to tell you. I was going to." I assured him.

"You'll have to take that up with her I think Mark, my friend." He suggested.

"I will when I get the chance to do so Pancho." I promised him grimly.

"As soon as possible Mark." He suggested to me once again with the unspoken sub text that I should find time to keep both my house and my women in order.

"So Mayhew is the one we want exhumed if they'll do it." I said eventually. Collecting my thoughts together. "How easy will it be to do that though I wonder?" I went on asking what I intended to be a rhetorical question.

"Very difficult I imagine." He said thoughtfully. Not seeing it that way at all, apparently "You would have to have a very convincing argument to get the body exhumed that's for certain. Perhaps it's time for me to take advice from my superiors."

"You have superiors you can ask?" I was surprised about that because Inspector Gomez hadn't seemed to have any when we'd had dealings before.

"Of course, doesn't everyone?" He sounded equally suprised that I should suggest he was a man alone, but then it could have been my experiences working with Chief Inspector Macdonald, who had beeen a man alone as far as I could see.

Not good to be as powerful as that, I'd always thought. It was probably why he seemed to see himself as someone more powerful than God almighty even.

"Who are you going to take it up with then?" I asked the Inspector inrerestedly.

"I think Superintendant Beamish would be the best man for me to go to to ask for advice about that Mark." He replied to my question thoughtfully.

"And where is he based, this Superintendant Beamish?" I asked the Inspector.

"At Carmathan police station, where I am too. In an office just across the way from mine, he is. I think I'd best get back there now and ask him."

"You'll let me know when you've done so?" I asked, uncertain as I asked the question, if he *would* keep me informed of his comings and goings like that.

"Of course!" He didn't seem to have any doubts on that score himself, even if I had some. "Why wouldnt I?"

"I'll wait for you to get in touch then. In the meantime, though, I think I'd best have a word or two with Alex about going over my head like that!"

CHAPTER NINE

"Why did you get in touch with Inspector Gomez without involving me at all?" I asked Alexandra a little bitterly when I'd run her to ground in her own front room after finally getting Inspector Gomez to leave my front room, and head back to his office in Carmarthen later that same morning.

"My daughter, who used to work at the hospital you were treated in, thought one of the nurses dealing with you was having a relationship with another woman." She replied sharply, speaking without a trace of remorse about her, it had to be said.

"So?" I'd suspected as much giving what Colin Croft, the man who'd fallen to his death whilst distributing library books in the hospital I had had been treated in, had hinted at when telling me his own story to match mine. "I can't see what that had got to do with getting in touch with him instead of with me first, Alexandra." I told her with a scowl of disapproval"

"I thought you might not be as quick to report that deviant behaviour as I was." She explained, or didn't really explain to me, because I still wasn't entirely sure in my mind why she had done what she had done when she had done it.

I proved that by asking her, "Why wouldn't I tell the authoritiesAlex?" as I revealed my total ignorance of her reasoning in this with that question I was sure.

"Because generally speaking men don't see lesbian behaviour in the same light as women do." She said as if that ought to have explained everything, but in reality only serving to confuse me even more than she had confused me before.

"Well they couldn't really could they, Alex, them being men after all." I commented eventually, having thought about what she'd just said to me.

"Men find it a turn on to see two women together." She said it as if it was a pertinent fact known to everyone. And to men in particular, all men in fact, she seemed to be suggesting with that remark of hers.

Not to me though as it happened. "Do we? Find seeing two women together a turnon" I questioned her take on life as she knew it, or had known it up until now.

"In my experience of men's fancies that they do." She said it as if that was a proven fact and I wouldn't dare to challenge her over.

"What experience?" I questioned her, because if it was a proven fact as far as she as concerned, it certainly wasn't a proven fact in my life or that of my friends.

"I do have a husband remember?" She reminded sharply as if it was something I would have been likely to forget, not that I would for a variety of reasons. Not least the fact it made or getting together like this, given our relative positions on Beazley Parish Council a little unwise perhaps.

"And your husband likes seeing two women performing together does he, Alex?" I questioned her take on life and all that went with it it seemed, sharply.

"He suggested to me once that a friend of mine and I got together in our bed!" She said irritably. Reliving that moment in her mind unhappily perhaps.

"You and you friend take him up on it?" I couldn't imagine that they would have done in the short experience I'd had of knowing her so far. She'd liked going to bed with a man too much for that to have been the case.

"Of course not!" She snapped back at me in case I might have entertained the thought that she would have done so. "What do you take me for, Mark, to ask such a question of me like that?"

"And anyway, I don't see, what's that got to do with you turning my experiences over to the police in the shape of Inspector Gomez and Superintendent Beamish?" I interrupted her flow, still completely bemused about her motive in doing that.

"Annie said that from her experience of working with her, she thought your nurse in black was having a relationship with another woman!" She said with venom in her voice as she glared at me as if I'd set the whole up for the two of them somehow. From her reaction I suspected she feared for her daughter's morals

72

in what to me she appeared to see as some sort of evil den of iniquity.

"Another of the nurses?" Again it wasn't a secret of any sort, to my way of thinking at least, that at least one and possibly three men, who were connected to the two women, had died because of this hidden relationship between them.

"Annie thought that was who the other woman was, another one of the nurses she'd had dealings with, but she wasn't sure that was the case."

"So in case I wasn't going to mention it to the police myself, you pre-empted me possibly failing in my duty as you saw it in doing so, by going to them yourself?" I spoke a little sharply in response at her judging me in that way without really knowing anything about me and my views on the subject.

"I did." She admitted apparently without the slightest trace of remorse to show for her misjudgement as I saw it.

"Actually there was a woman who was a lesbian in love with a woman who wasn't a lesbian, who I also loved, who tried to get her to kill me once, but it was the woman I was in love with who got killled instead. I said, remembering.

"By the lesbian?" She demanded. A bit surprised by the revelation I assumed.

"By somebody else as it happened," I replied, "by a policeman involved with the case as it happened, but all related to my rival in this being a lesbian. I didn't take against all lesbians as a result of it though, or try to get into bed with her either!"

"You didn't?" Alex asked, as if she wasn't sure whether to believe me or not.

"I didn't." I assured her, still remembering the occasion sadly and all that had happened to me since.

"You've led a very adventurous life for a parish clerk haven't you?" Alex said in a surprised tone of voice, as if she thought my behaviour as deviant as being a lesbian was to her. "How many other murders have you been involved in. I thought the body you found in the woods was the only on."

"Well it wasn't, but that's a different story. The point is that lesbian or not, I would have gone to the police about the two women because I think one of them at least committed a murder, maybe even three murders between them," I spoke no more than the truth when I said it, having already set the whole thing going as far as I could see, "but I didn't get the chance to go either way with it did I thanks to you not trusting me?"

"So you say," She, agreed, looking hard at me as she posed her question, "but would you really have done that, Mark, if I hadn't prompted you by going to the police about what you believed had happened first?"

"That's hardly the point now is it." I pointed out to her pertinently. "Anyway, I think the point in all this is not whether or not they're

74

lesbians, but whether or not they killed one or both of their husbands because of their relationship, or neither of them at all when it came down to it."

"And whether or not one of them also pushed the library man down the stairs to his death after seeing them together!" Alexandra agreed. "Or allegedly pushed him down the stairs to his death, anyway!" She said in conclusion.

"None of which is going to be easy to prove unless one of them breaks under pressure and reveals all, and tells us how it all happened as a result of my interest." I pointed out to my companion.

"Nor will it be easy to prove that either of the men died under circumstances suspicious enough to get the police to investigate further." My sometime bedtime companion came on line at that pont with a flourish.

"Especially as one of them was cremated." I agreed with what she was saying to me about it.

"One was cremated," She agreed, obviously still thinking the thing through as she did so, because she continued pertinently after a moment, "thereby taking any possible proof of foul play in occurred to the furnace with him!"

"It would be easier to find out the truth whatever it as if only one of these women was involved in the murders and the other knew nothing about it." Alexandra said thoughtfully, picking up on what I had suggested and running with it.

"Explain to me how you wouldn't know about your lover getting your husbands out of the way so they could live together without complications, without being involved in it yourself?" I asked my companion more than a litle doubtfully.

"Do they live together these women were pursuing so diligently Mark." She countered my question with a question of her own to follow mine up at that point.

"I'm afraid I don't know." I had to admit reluctantly after a little thought on the subject had revealed that I really didn't have the faintest idea about that.

"So what is the police, in the form of Inspector Gomez's next move, going to be to put that right Mark?" She carried on with another question at that point.

"To look into how the library man came to fall down those stairs," I replied, "Someone might have seen something surely? They can't all have been asleep at the moment when it was happening like I was it seems."

"Someone must have seen something, heard something, or heard the culprits talking about it in a huddle somewhere." She agreed with my supposition.

"If the police and us stir things up enough for them by looking into the two death's it might cause a split between the two women were they both involved or only one of them doing it on her own with the other not knowing anything about it." I suggested what our next course of action ought to be.

"And the same with the man who fell downstairs to his death." I continued thoughtfully. So that was what we decided to do next did and would have done if events hadn't conspired to prevent it.

CHAPTER TEN

In light of the fact I thought Alexandra
Merrydew had over reached herself by going to
see Inspector Gomez to tell him about what her
daughter had told her about the women we
suspected of murdering their husbands, I hadn't
told her about the police applying to the
Coroners Court for permission the exhume
Christopher Mayhew's body and examine it for
any traces of foul play in the course of his
operation bringing about his untimely death in
the first place.

I had never had to attend a coroner's court
on behalf of any of the parish councils I'd
worked for - a lot of planning meetings
attended over the years, and a site meeting or
two to do with someone wanting to build an
affordable house in their garden, but that was it,
in my life as a parish clerk.

Since the proceedings carried on at
coroners' courts were open to the public,
however, and this was to be a completely new
experience for me, even though I wouldn't
needed to take part in any proceedings myself,
as I had done when finding Benny Bartletts
body that time, I went along to the court
anyway. Cadging a lift to it in the
superintendent's car rather than driving there in
my own.

Most folk who adopt the Coroners role in
life are usually either lawyers or doctors with a

minimum of five years' experience under their belts.

I didn't know if that was the case with the Coroner who ran the court at Shrewsbury or not, but by the look of him he could have been in either category.

In most cases, it is a doctor, or the police, who refer a death to the coroner to be examined further by him. And then for him to direct whether or not any further action needed to be taken after the referral has been completed.

That was what had happened here as I knew, having been part of proceedings since the whole thing had begun. The death had been referred to the coroner both because it had been unexpected, as well as being unnatural and suspicious, probably with an unintended, on the part of the patient anyway, drug overdose being involved to bring about the death.

Also, it had occurred during, or soon after, a hospital procedure, such as surgery, and deaths under those circumstances are always passed on to the district coroner for his ruling on what was or wasn't to be done about it if anything was going to be.

Superintendent Beamish, the man whose car I was travelling in, was the man of high enough rank based at the local police station, in this case based at Caernarfon Police Station to be able to request that action be taken to exhume the body, who attended the coroner's court on our behalf.

That was held at Shrewsbury Police Station, so was very convenient for him to go to to put that request forward and be granted a licence, if the coroner so directed, to exhume the body of the unfortunate Christopher Mayhew, who was the man whose body had been buried in a churchyard, whilst Edward Evans had been the one whose body had been cremated, so no trace of his mortal remains had survived to be exhumed.

I made myself known to the officiating clerk when I got to the court, just in case I was needed for any reason, though I didn't expect to be as I hadn't witnessed anything in regard to the unexplained deaths as I had on that previous occasion when reporting on the body of Benny Bartlett I'd found murdered in the woods, then sat at the back of the room in case I was called to give evidence anyway, even though I wasn't expecting to be summoned for any reason.

Looking around the room to see who else was attending the inquest, I noticed that there was no one there apart from people I already knew as members of the parish council I worked for. I had thought Alexandra Merrydew might be there out of interest, even though she hadn't said she would be.

No relatives, friends or neighbours from the village where he had lived were anywhere in evidence as far as I could see, something that was often the case in my experience.

The coroner began by explaining that because the police thought, as a result of suspicions put to them by Colin Croft, who had been an unpaid volunteer taking library books around St Bartholomew's hospital in Hereford for patients unable to leave their beds to borrow for however long they were there.

Colin Croft was someone who had subsequently died himself by falling down several flights of stairs at St Bartholomew's hospital, though it was still uncertain whether he had fallen accidently or been pushed. That was because of the suspicions first aired by Colin Croft, that there was a strong possibility that two men who had died during operations carried out at the hospital during fairly recent times, which shouldn't have led to either patient dying during the proceedings that they had, in fact, died.

One of the men who died had been cremated shortly afterwards, so no trace of his body remained to be exhumed. The police had, however decided to investigate the possibility of foul play further, by exhuming the body of the other man, who had been buried, not cremated to see if there were any traces about the remains which suggested the foul play bringing about the premature death of the man, as the unfortunate Colin Croft had told me, had been the case.

There were several nurses present to be called as witnesses if needed for that purpose, amongst whom was the one I remembered with some bitterness as being the one who had summarily ejected me from the hospital ahead of schedule and without referring to any higher authority on my behalf. The nurse in black of painful memory.

Sister Evans was obviously not taken with being questioned strongly in this way by anyone who dared to doubt her professional integrity in any way as the coroner appeared to do to her.

"Mr Mayhew and Mr Evans, the two patients who died, could you say for certain that there wasn't any negligence on the part of you nurses that that happened?" The Coroner asked what seemed a reasonable question to me, and probably to everyone else in the court too, I'd imagine, but not to Sister Evans apparently, if the way she responded could be taken as a guide.

"Of course not!" She declared forcefully, nostrils flaring as she did so, in a way I remembered only too well from my incarceration in the hospital. "Whatever might have been suggested to you by a man with an axe to grind, I can assure you that they both had the best treatment available to them at the time!"

"I see from the records that they died a few months between the two deaths." The coroner interjected at that point as Sister Evans seemed to have run out of steam in her slagging off of the library man, Colin Croft. "Did any other deaths occur during that same period of time Sister Evans?"

"It's a hospital." Sister Evans, nostrils flared in anger again, she obviously hadn't run out of steam in her tirade, just pausing whilst she regrouped for a moment, before continuing with it. "You remember Covid don't you?" She asked the coroner scathingly. "Lots of people died during that same period of time as I recall. We've just come out of a covid pandemic haven't we for heaven's sake!"

"But not as a result of operations they ought to have come through without problem wouldn't you say?" The coroner pointed out to Sister Evans mildly in response to the charges she'd levelled at the authorities and him in particular.

"I *wouldn't* say!" Sister Evans disputed his mild remark angrily. Obviously just working herself up to her second blast at him. "This seems to me to be just another ill considered attack on the NHS and its nurses!"

"I'm sorry you see it that way Sister Evans." The coroner still tried to appear mild in his responses to her venom, in light of her spirited defence of NHS staff in general and of those involved in the covid pandemic in particular.

"In what other way do you expect me to see it?" She must have known she was onto a loser in this despite her spirited defence of all she stood for.

Did she know what the police were going to find out when the body was exhumed? If she *was* guilty of the murder, as we all knew the man *had* been murdered she must have done.

If innocent of murder and just guilty of overreacting to the presence of men in general it in her world it seemed to me, it would leave the police, and me perhaps, with eggs on our faces after all this had ended.

Perhaps it was just because of the way I'd suffered at her hands whilst having to helplessly submit to her ministrations whilst in that hospital, but somehow I doubted if that was going to be the case that she would prove to have been the helpless victim of life when this was all over.

The coroner obviously saw things in the same way as the police and I did, because he summed the proceedings up by saying. "I think on consideration that I am going to allow the police their licence to exhume the body of the man who was buried, not cremated, Mr Mayhew, and then we'll know if he died as a result of malpractice or not!"

CHAPTER ELEVEN

Of course, getting the coroner to grant a licence to have the body of Christopher Mayhew exhumed turned out to be the easy part in the proceedings.

Quickly followed by more difficult questions, because it led to questions such as what happens when a body is exhumed, is a particular person required to do it being asked? Is anyone allowed to do it? Or must a particular undertaker take it on? Does an exhumed body have to be taken to a particular morgue to be examined? How long does it take for the authorities to report back afterwards?

"You're a parish clerk" Superintendent Beamish pointed out to me as if I might have forgotten that small detail in my life as we were making the short journey down the stairs from the coroner's court to his office in Shrewsbury Police Station. "So you ought to know who to get to exhume a body once the coroner has granted the petitioner permission."

His voice dared me not to know the answer to that. But, "I do as it happens." I told him with more certainty in my voice than I felt in all honesty it had to be said. Because I had had previous experience of working for a parish council which had been involved in just such an event as I recalled, whilst I was working for them as their clerk.

"The removal of a dead body from the ground after it has been buried is known as exhumation." I went on in my parish clerk reading out the minutes at a meeting, voice.

"In Ireland, exhumation can only take place in certain circumstances. There the person who has died must be treated with respect, and the privacy of their family and friends must be protected at all times.

Exumation for family reasons such as the family of a deceased person wanting the remains to be moved to another burial ground was one situation I'd come upon in the past. Not for public health reasons, nor for a cemetery is being moved for any reason.

Finally, though, there was the case as with our body, of the Minister for Justice ordering an exhumation as part of a criminal investigation.

Exhumation licences are issued by whichever local authority is responsible for the parish in which the body has been buried. You should ask that local authority for an application form and return the completed form with the fee required, and copy of the death certificate of the deceased person."

"Anything else required?" Superintendent Beamish asked, as I paused in my account to gather my thoughts.

"The local authority may ask us for further documentation if they feel it is needed." I continued eventually. "In some instances a local authority may refuse an exhumation licence because, the consent of the next of kin has not been given, the burial plot cannot be identified, or because the remains lie unidentified in a common plot, such as in the burial plot of a religious order of some sort.

Due respect to the person who died cannot always be guaranteed during the process of exhuming a body, unfortunately. Especially if the remains to be exhumed are located below a body that is not to be exhumed at the same time, public health and decency cannot be protected, or ground conditions in the graveyard would make an exhumation difficult or unsafe.

In all those cases conditions attached to the exhumation licence mean that they cannot be complied with.

After your local authority has granted an exhumation licence, *if* they grant you an exhumation licence, exhumation must take place within twelve months, and there must be an Environmental Health Officer present at the exhumation.

This is to ensure that all procedures are complied with and everyone present shows respect to the deceased person at all times. The Environmental Health Officer must be notified of the time, date and place of exhumation at least five working days before the exhumation. Screens are placed around the existing grave to protect the exhumation from being in the public view whilst it is going on.

If necessary, a bigger area of the graveyard than the grave area itself is cordoned off to ensure privacy. Workers must treat the neighbouring burial plots with care. Disinfectants and disposable protective clothing must be available to workers carrying out the work and disposed of safely after the exhumation.

The exhumed remains, including the existing casket, are placed in a new casket. Any other remains in the same burial plot that may have been disturbed during the exhumation are reburied with respect."

"There is more?" Superintendent Beamish asked as I paused to gather my thought a final time for a final rush of information required, and I expect that he hoped for a minute I was done.

"When the local authority receives your request for an exhumation, the Environmental Health Officer inspects the grave of the deceased person and may ask the cemetery managers and the undertakers for further information as required. The Environmental Health Officer attends and supervises the exhumation to ensure that respect for the deceased person is maintained and that public health is protected. If the remains are to be reburied in the same local authority area, the Environmental Health Officer also supervises the reburial. If the remains are to be reburied elsewhere, the Environmental Health Officer will ensure that the appropriate local authority receives all the details it needs.

The Institutional Burials Act gives the Government the power to appoint a Director of

Authorized Intervention to oversee the recovery of the remains of people who were buried on the grounds of institutions that were controlled or funded by the state. In that case The Director will be assisted by an Advisory Board.

The purpose of the Act is to give the Director the authority to excavate the site, to recover human remains and to analyse those remains. To identify the remains through DNA matching where possible, to return the remains to family members or give the deceased persons a respectful burial in line with their family's wishes….."

"How long does all this take?" Superintendent Beamish asked, looking a little shell shocked by the amount of information I'd blasted him with, but I carried on imparting it to him anyway.

"A post-mortem must be carried out as soon as possible, usually within two to three working days of the body being exhumed. In some cases, it may be possible for it to take place within twenty four hours….."

"The post-mortem will take place in an examination room that looks similar to an operating theatre and has been licensed for the purpose." Inspector Gomez got in on the act at that point as I took a back seat in proceedings now, my role as a purveyor of information come to an end.

"The examination room will be licensed and inspected by the HTA beforehand. During the procedure, the deceased person's body will be opened and the organs removed for examination to see if there are any signs of foul play involving them to report back to us about. Some organs need to be examined in close detail during a post-mortem. These investigations can take several weeks to complete. The pathologist will return the organs to the body after the post-mortem has been completed.

"We arranged for Nevilles, who are our nearest local undertakers, to make all the arrangements necessary for the body to exhumed as quickly as possible and with the greatest respect before taking to the morgue for the post mortem...."

"They've been told they have to screen the area from being overseen by anyone using the churchyard for any other purpose?" Superintendent Beamish interrupted his underling at that point, to check that all the arrangements which would have been arranged by him had been arranged.

"They have. ..." That underling wasn't allowed to say very much more before being interrupted again".....

"What time of day are they going to doing it?" Superintendent Beamish wanted to know next.

"Apparently late morning is the time of day when there's the least numbers of passers by" I was able to get in my own bit of information then which I'd gleaned from personal experience.

"What are they going to say if anyone asks what they are doing and why they're doing it?" The superintendent was revealing himself to be a worrier of the first order. "It might happen."

"They can tell people what they are doing." Inspector Gomez replied matter of factly. "It will be fairly obvious what they are doing I would have thought, but the people doing the digging ought to say if asked, that they don't know why they are doing it."

"And if those asking difficult questions persist?" Superintendent Beamish continued not to know the obvious as far as the rest of us could see.

"Refer them to me." Inspector Gomez said stoutly. "It will depend on whose action the question is about, what answer I'll give them. Once the body's dug up the undertakers are going to put it into a coffin and take it to the morgue to be examined for signs of foul play."

"And afterwards?" I asked, as I felt I had the right to do, having set all this business in motion in the first place.

"It depends on what the outcome of the post mortem is." Superintendent Beamish replied. "We might have to reinter it, or keep it in cold storage pending a court case to prosecute someone for murder."

"Will it come to that do you think?" I asked, still amazed that something I had set in motion in the first place had got to this point eventually.

"It will definitely come to that!" Inspector Gomez had no doubt on that score it seemed to me.

"Have we told the victims wife what we're doing?" Superintendent Beamish asked at that point.

"It must almost certainly have been her did for him, if anyone did," Inspector Gomez said matter-of-factly, "she must already know what the outcome of our investigation is likely to be! Unless we're wrong about all this, of course!"

"And if we *are* wrong and it *wasn't* her?" Superintendent Beamish suggested what was an impossibility as far as the rest of us were concerned.

"It had to be her did for him if anyone did surely! What would anyone else have to gain by murdering after all"? I put in my two penneth at that point.

"Perhaps it will all turn out that he died of natural causes not as a result of him being murdered." Superintendent Beamish, the eternal pessimist, suggested.

"Perhaps." Inspector Gomez replied, but not as if he really meant that in even the slightest degree.

"You don't think so?" The superintendent asked his second in command in a surprised tone of voice.

"I don't think so." That one replied. "She should get a term to serve in prison if she's guilty and if we can prove it of course."

"We just got the report from the morgue." Superintendent Beamish was reading something which had just come up on his computer.

"What did it say?" I was as interested in that outcome as Gomez was, but it was him who actually asked the question on his chief.

"That the body contained traces of a drug which shouldn't have been there," Beamish was still reading his screen excitedly, "and that undoubtedly resulted in the victim dying a premature death rather than recovering from his operation and going on to live a full and happy life as he would otherwise have done." His voice trailed off a bit as he continued to read his screen.

"On the strength of that are we intending to charge the man's wife with carrying out that murder?" Inspector Gomez asked.

"We most certainly are!" Superintendent Beamish assured him.

"A term in prison will undoubtedly follow those charges if she's found guilty of them," Gomez remarked thoughtfully.

"I would have thought though that both of them must have known what was going down and be equally guilty of the crime!" He mused on the possibilities presented by the results.

"Now we know for certain, I guess it's time to bring in one of the women and try to be separated from each other and their stories." Superintendent Beamish was still reading his computer screen as if he couldn't believe what it was telling him, despite it being the outcome the three of us had expected.

"The one who we just proved husband was poisoned would probably be the best to start on." Inspector Gomez suggested. "Tell her we've proved her husband was murdered for starters and see what she has to say about it. She might give her friend up as being the one who carried out the crime."

"Unlikely, I think," Beamish disputed the others suggestion with a shake of his head, "But I'll call her into my office for a friendly chat in the light of what we've just found out, anyway, and see where that leads us to." "Hopefully, if you call her into the station we'll find out once and for all." I commented at that point.

"Perhaps," the policemen replied as if they didn't really expect such an outcome as we all set out to play our own parts in setting up that outcome.

CHAPTER TWELVE

"Do you have anything to say about the charge put forward that you husband didn't die a natural death?" Monday morning at Carmarthen Police Station, and Jay Lane who had been summoned to meet Inspector Gomez there to answer questions about her possible involvement in the three alleged murders which had taken place at St Bartholomew's hospital in Hereford.

"He was my partner actually, not my husband, but charge! What charge?" Jay, dressed in a grey trouser suit for the occasion, having climbed the three flight of stairs it took to get to the office the inspector was using, and was therefore a little breathless as a result, glared an all encompassing glare which took in the entire office, not just the desk being used by Gomez.

"Put forward by whom?" She demanded of him a little haughtily though she was already fully aware of the answer to that question of course.

"By Colin Croft, who was going to out you to Mark Montgomery who was a patient in the hospital at the time, but got distracted at a vital moment, and then fell to his death down several flights of stairs before he was able to finish what he'd been about to say to Mr Montgomery." Inspector Gomez replied.

"Did he actually mention my husband by name when making these allegations?" Jay asked pertinently. Sure that he hadn't done anything of the sort. Glaring at the inspector across the expanse of his desk in his office there at the police station.

"No," Inspector Gomez admitted to her after thought, "he just said that what in his opinion were two suspicious deaths which had gone unreported. Men, who according to Mr Croft, had died on the operating table who in his opinion shouldn't have done, and wouldn't have done, if their operations hadn't been tampered with in some way at the time, by those in the know."

"Mr Croft was a trained medical practitioner of some sort I take it?" Jay Lane, who knew perfectly well that that certainly wasn't the case," asked Inspector Gomez haughtily, glaring at him all the while as she did so.

"I'm afraid he wasn't, Mrs Lane," The police officer admitted uneasily, well aware that this wasn't going to be an easy interview for him. It wasn't. Nothing like one in fact!

"And on the strength of that unsubstantiated story you decided to bring me in for questioning!" Jay declared, eyes blazing at the police officer. "I think it might be a case of all the men in this case ganging up on two women they know to be lesbians! What do you think inspector?" She demanded of that man.

"Nothing of the sort Mrs Lane!" That one refuted the charge strongly. " In actual fact, in light of our informants suspicions we asked you to come here for a chat to see if there might a case for further investigation of them on our part, nothing more than that, I promise you."

She couldn't see from her position across the desk from him that Inspector Gomez had his fingers firmly crossed behind his back as he said it, "that is why we've brought you in here for questioning." He paused, looking at the woman in front of him uneasily as she raised a silencing hand to him.

"I think you need to think very carefully before you proceed with this matter Inspector Gomez" Jay Lane declared stoutly, holding her ground in their tussle as she did so, "you might just find yourself facing charges of your own about police misrepresentation if you're not very careful you know!"

"You deny it then?" Inspector Gomez asked her, knowing full well what her response to all this was going to be.

"Of course I deny it Inspector!" She declared firmly, nostrils flaring in anger again as she did so.

"And supposing we move to have your husband's body exhumed in order to find out if there were any suspicious circumstances surrounding his death?" He asked the woman sitting opposite him threateningly.

The inspector, was fully aware that had already happened and that, by means of the autopsy she didn't know the police had already secretly carried out, revealing drugs in his body which shouldn't have been there under normal circumstances, the deceased had already been found to have been murdered.

The fact that the woman didn't know this, suggested a possible scenario, which would allow her the opportunity to admit to it all if she chose to do so, thereby saving the public the expense of a trial by so doing.

"Then you'll be wasting your time and a lot of public money by doing so," Jay Lane declined to make any such public spirited gesture to the police officer, "because there certainly weren't any!"

"Colin Croft certainly thought that there were." Inspector Gomez pointed out to the woman in front of him with a secret smile she couldn't fathom, though it irritated her beyond belief to be on the receiving end of it like that.

"Colin Croft was a bitter old man with a grudge against women, inspector, though Lord knows why he had one. Perhaps his mother misused him at some time." Jay Lane hazarded a reason as to why the man who distributed the library books to patients in the hospital, before coming to a untimely end the way he had, might have disliked women in general and her and her friend in particular. "You'll be backing a loser if you hitch yourself to that wagon, I fear inspector!"

"What about Annie Obrien? She was a woman. Did she have a grudge about women in general too and you and your friend in particular as well, Mrs Lane? Is that why she came forward with information about you both when we asked for it" Inspector Gomez enquired of her.

"Annie Obrien? I don't think I know the name!" Did Jay Lane *really* not know, or was she just playing for time with that denial?

"She was a nurse at the hospital a little while ago." Inspector Gomez filled in the particulars of his other witness. "A woman just like you are, and a nurse too at one time at your hospital too, so you can't say it's a case of all boys together if she also says she was there when Colin Croft was pushed down those stairs to his death."

"And does she say it?" Jay Lane asked the inspector, getting to her feet so suddenly her chair fell over behind her, as she made moves to quit that office she had found herself hating before someone made a move to arrest her and keep her there against her will. As she feared might happen.

"She does I'm afraid." Inspector Gomez said sadly. Looking at her across the width of his desk.

"Well I still deny your suggestion categorically!" Jay assured him as she left, "and I know Lou will too when you put it to her. You *are* putting it to her as well I assume?" She asked as she headed out of the door and down the stairs.

"Naturally we are," The inspector assured her with a frown, "we were just giving you to respond to the charges first!" He watched as the door of the superintendent's office swung closed behind her with an audible click.

"When they find out we actually know that Mr Mayhew at least died as a result of her and her partners intervention to shorten his life considerably, her attitude will change." Superintendent Beamish spoke from the back of the room as the doors swung closed behind the departing suspect.

"You think that?" Inspector Gomez said doubtfully, as he turned towards his chief.

"I really think that!" That one said stoutly in the face of the other's denial.

"I'm surprised no one has told them yet what we were doing in the churchyard the other day." Superintendent Beamish commented thoughtfully.

"Digging her husband up and taking him off to the morgue for examination?" Inspector Gomez agreed. "Perhaps they were unpopular in their village for whatever reason, so nobody told them."

"Perhaps folk hope they'll be brought to justice and get their comeuppance in the hands of the police. For what they did to their husbands." The superintendent continued.

"Perhaps." Inspector Gomez agreed again, but not with any conviction in his voice.

CHAPTER THIRTEEN

"What are we going to do with regard to what the Lane woman just said to us about the other woman being responsible for all that happened at the hospital with regard to the two men who died there?" Inspector Pancho Gomez asked his superior officer, soon after the woman in question had departed, seemingly seething with indignation. Whether it was righteous indignation, or otherwise, had yet to be established.

"We know that the autopsy proved there had been foul play in regard to the body we were able to have examined by the pathologist," Superintendent Beamish replied, without actually answering the question he'd been asked, "that of her husband, or partner or whatever he was to her."

"She doesn't know we know though does she" The Inspector pointed out to his chief a little thoughtfully at that point. "That we had the body exhumed and had it examined by a forensic expert?" Beamish dotted the is and crossed the ts of his underling as it was his right to do. "No she doesn't know that, I guess."

"I can't believe word didn't get around in their village and back to the two women when we had the man's grave fenced off and the undertakers we'd instructed, were digging up the body." I commented pertinently to the two policemen from the seat I'd taken over at the other side of their office.

"Those two women obviously aren't popular in their village for that to have been the case." Superintendent Beamish summed up the situation as he saw it thoughtfully from his seat at the desk.

"You think their sexual proclivities, if generally known, might have had something to do with it?" Inspector Gomez summed up the situation as he saw it candidly for us others in the office.

"It's possible." Superintendent Beamish agreed with him, adding a little thoughtfully as he did so, "In any case I think we need to take advice from someone as to what we ought to do next."

"We need to bring the other woman in for questioning for a start." Gomez agreed, adding his own suggestion to the mix. "We only have her friend's version of what went down between them."

"The one who's the sister at the hospital where it all happened you mean?" I asked, though I knew full well to whom he was referring with his remark.

"I do." Pablo Gomez agreed with his superior officer.

"We already know what her attitude is going to be don't we?" Superintendent Beamish pointed out to us others involved. "She already made that very clear at the coroners court wouldn't you say?"

"We bring her in anyway!" Gomez said pugnaciously, "like we did with the other one, and then we tell her that her friend put the finger on her for both of the murders the way she did!"

"And then see if she cracks?" I asked the two men.

"And then see if she cracks!" Pablo Gomez agreed, in pugnacious mood again.

"I doubt that she will." I pointed out to the others with a certainty born of my treatment in the hands of the woman whilst I was a patient and she was a nurse at the hospital in Hereford I'd been treated in.

"I doubt that she will either." Superintendent Beamish, with less personal experience to draw on nevertheless agreed with my assessment of things it seemed from that certainty he stated.

"Even if we bring up the man who fell to his death down the stairs!" Inspector Gomez also agreed with the two of us about what Mrs Evans was likely to do by way of response to our charges.

"Even if we bring up the man who fell to his death down the stairs." I thought back to the event when I'd been incarcerated in that hospital which had begun it all as far as I was concerned.

"I think we need to be careful she doesn't just clam up on us if we take that tack with her," Superintendent Beamish commented to the pair of us thoughtfully, "go defensive on us straight away, and tell us nothing in the end."

"You think she might Stone Wall us do you?" I said speculative to the other man.

"I think she might well Stone Wall us." Superintendent Beamish agreed.

"Supposing we try telling her her friend told on her in every detail?" Inspector Gomez suggested a possible way of prompting the outcome we were hoping for. "Putting the blame for everything that happened firmly on her?"

"You think she'll believe that?" I asked. I didn't believe that it *would* happen that easily myself, but felt I had to suggest the possibility to the others anyway.

"Probably not." Inspector Gomez, who had the same view as me on the subject, replied sadly.

As did Superintendent Beamish it seemed. "I'll take advice from higher authority and report back to you tomorrow." Superintendent Beamish promised us jointly.

"Okay." Gomez agreed for the pair of us, but that didn't have to happen, because later the same day, he was told there was someone wanting to speak to him on Zoom, even though he hadn't arranged such a meeting, and when he turned his machine on and looked into the camera lense he found Jay Lane smiling back at him a little uncertainly.

CHAPTER FOURTEEN

Inspector Gomez had thought his investigations into the St Bartholomew's Hospital murders was done for the day until he was told there was someone wanting to speak to him on Zoom, even though he hadn't arranged such a meeting, and when he turned his machine on and looked into the camera found Jay Lane smiling back at him a little uncertainly.

"I want to retract what I told you before," she told him at last when they had greeted each other and she was sure it was him on the other side of the Zoom camera, not the Superintendent, nor me in particular I was sure.

She would have recognised us as being considerably less sympathetic recipients of her reaching out to the police force in that fashion I was sure.

"What do you want to retract?" Pablo Gomez asked her interestedly, wishing one of the other two of us on the investigative team were within earshot of what was going down with her.

"What I said about the men who died after their operations failed..." her voice tailed off a little at that point, as if she was uncertain how to, or if to, continue with what she was saying to him.

"Yes?" He prompted as if her voice tailing off at that point was a prelude to her not continuing her story at all. Which was what he feared might happen. "…..One of them being my husband." She continued at last, having passed to regroup her thoughts, not to end her account altogether.

"Yes?" Inspector Gomez prompted the reluctant witness questioningly again.

"I'm admitting now that I did know what was going on," her words were coming out in a rush now that she'd decided to speak it seemed, "but it was my partner, Lou who set it up and carried them out…."

"Lou Evans you mean? Is she the person you're talking about" Inspector Gomez interrupted at that point, so he could be sure it was the right Lou she was talking about, just in case we'd got it wrong. Or part of it wrong at least.

Jay Lane seemed a bit put out by the need for further information, pausing for a moment before answering it. "Lou Evans? ……Yes of course! You don't think I have more than one partner do you?" She snapped her response.

"How did she do it?" Pablo Gomez asked, "killing someone like that wasn't an easy thing for her to do I imagine."

She didn't answer his question immediately, well not at all actually as it happened, going on to tell him something that he already knew well enough. Something that we all knew only too well, me especially as it happened.

"You *do* know that she works at the hospital I suppose?" she asked what could only have been meant as a rhetorical question, because it was obvious that we did.

"Yes." He agreed. Waiting for her to continue without any prompting on his part which someone, her partner came instantly to mind, might later use to claim he was leading a witness.

"She's a nurse there…." She paused again as if to consider what she was saying to the police officer through the Zoom lense, pausing to gather her thoughts on the subject' perhaps.

"We know." He told her, because we did. Only too well unfortunately in my personal experience of the woman it had to be said. Frantic texting on his part on his mobile phone, had brought the superintendent to join him now.

"Do you work there too?" That one asked. Not having the slightest idea whether she could see him too on the screen of her Zoom but needing to keep the conversation going.

Whether she could see him or not she answered the question he'd asked almost without any pause on her part. "I used to, but not anymore." She said.

"Why is that?" Superintendent Beamish asked as if he didn't already know.

"Because Lou took advantage of me in her car in the woods one summers evening." She replied candidly. "Seduced me on the back seat of her car in the woods. There's no other word for what she did to me. I wasn't that way inclined at all, or didn't think I was until then anyway. And she's still the only other woman I've ever been with!" She told the two police officers sadly.

"Is she?" Beamish replied. Having no possible means of testing the veracity of his suspects story.

"In the first flush of our relationship I thought I was in love with her," Jay Lane replied sadly, "even though I knew most people wouldn't approve in the slightest of what we were doing together every chance we got."

"Because you're both women?" Superintendent Beamish asked, keeping the conversation going, fully aware of what the reply to his question would be.

"Because we're both women." Jay Lane agreed sadly again with what he'd said.

"So what are you retracting about your previous statement?" Inspector Gomez asked doubtfully, reading through what he'd written down as being her new statement according to her, "It all seems pretty much what you told me before as far as I can see you know, having looked through it again."

"Saying you didn't know anything about it?" Beamish continued with the line of questioning his second in command had begun. "The two murders which you say your partner carried out and which you knew nothing about!"

"I *didn't* know about them…" Jay Lane paused as if uncertain now she had begun it, how to continue with her denial of any sort of complicity in what had gone down.

"Yes?" Superintendent Beamish prompted from behind Inspector Gomez's face on the screen. Interested in getting things cleared up if they could.

"I didn't know she was doing all that other stuff as well." Jay Lane answered his leading question, very reluctantly it seemed to the two men listening.

"Other stuff? " Beamish prompted the reluctant witness again. "I knew we were having sex together, of course, how could I not know that if I was a participant, a willing participant in that, but not that Lou was killing people as well." She replied baldly.

"Your husbands?" Gomez, his face still filling the screen of the Zoom, asked what was a very pertinent question as far as the investigation being carried out by the police department was concerned.

"Our husbands." Jay Lane agreed, sadly it seemed to the two police officers involved. "I found out afterwards that she had killed both of them to get them out of the way of our relationship, and make us living together easier."

"So why have you come to us now with your story, Ms Lane?" Inspector Pablo Gomez asked the woman filling his screen at that moment pointedly.

"Because its got to stop." She replied sadly to his screen again. "I know if you do have my partner Christopher Mayhew's body exhumed there will be traces of a narcotic substance in it which killed him, I'm afraid!"

"How did it come to be there?" Superintendent Beamish knew already that there had been traces of a narcotic substance in the body when exhumed, but not a confession from either of the women as to how it came to be there.

"Lou procured the drugs she used from the poison cupboard in the hospital where I used to work but don't anymore and she still does." Jay Lane said, but it wasn't said directly to the screen, but in a matter of fact kind of way.

"And you are telling us this Ms Lane, for what reason would you say?" Superintendent Beamish, it seemed, was going for the kill in the matter.

"Because she's got to be stopped!" Jay Lane declared angrily. "The woman is out of control! She takes advantage of me sexually every chance she gets!"

"You need to come to the station and repeat all you've just been telling me after setting it down in writing and reading it though carefully." Inspector Gomez advised the woman they hopped would be to be their star witness in court when it came to court appearances by any of the of the three of them.

"I'll do it tomorrow." She replied sadly. No longer concentrating on the screen in front of her it seemed to us who were simply there as observers.

"It might be better to come here at once!" Superintendent Beamish agreed with his second in command in that matter, even if he agreed with nothing else.

Fearing this star witness of theirs might wriggle though their fingers yet, if given just half a chance of wriggling free from what she'd agreed to in this late stage of proceedings, both sought to make sure she wasn't free to do any such thing.

"I'll come tomorrow." Jay Lane, the police forces potential star witness, perhaps suddenly aware of the ordeal before her if she went though with the things she'd just agreed to, prevaricated strongly at that point.

"This evening would be better." Inspector Gomez, also fully aware of the ordeal in front of their star witness if she carried on with what she'd agree to, also disagreed strongly with her take on things.

"I'll come tomorrow!" She continued to prevaricate, turning her Zoom camera off without warning, so the screen went dead on them.

CHAPTER FIFTEEN

"I think we need to include a female police officer in the team when we interview Mrs Evans or she's going to cry prejudice in a very loud voice!" Inspector Gomez suggested to his chief.

"It's my experience in this case that the women we meet up with are more prejudiced against women who are lesbians than any man could be. I do agree with you in principle though." Superintendent Beamish agreed.

"Who did you have in mind though? Someone who already works at the station? I must confess no one amongst the women based at the station have come instantly into my mind!"

"There's a sergeant based here I've had a few dealings with over the years. Phyllis Fernackerly is her name." The Inspector said matter of factly.

"And you think she'd be the person for the job?" Superintendent Beamish asked his underling.

"I do." That one said with certainty. A shade too much certainty perhaps.

"Didn't she get involved with that inspector they're trying to get rid of because of all the criminal activities he's been part of over the years." Beamish pointed out to his underling. "Meryoneth Jones was his name wasn't it? Is he still involved in those activities which were set up by his cousin Blodwyn something or other, who he worked with when she was a receptionist at a hotel in the hills as far as I recall!"

"You have a very good memory to remember all that!" Inspector Gomez not at all happy that he should be so well informed, remarked looking at his superior officer questioningly.

"Only because it involved criminal activities on the part of a police officer." Superintendent Beamish justified his interest in the matter. "I really can't stand that sort of thing." He added.

It was day or two later and I was with the two police officers trying to work out what we should do next to bring our two murders to justice. I had just made the coffee as I often did at parish council meetings whilst we pondered on what to do next.

"Phyllis Fernankerly her name was, the sergeant she was working with at the time and she was cleared of any involvement with what he was doing other than turning a blind eye where a superior officer was concerned as it happens, something a lot of us have been guilty of doing over the years I'm sure, but people have been treating her as if she had been in with him, nevertheless." Inspector Gomez was finishing his story.

I wasn't sure I liked being lumped in with folk turning blind eyes at that point because it was something I had never guilty of, especially

when working with Chief Inspector
Macdonald.

"So you told her you'd see her alright?"
Superintendent Beamish sounded a little bit
critical of the Inspector, and his part in things,
it had to be said

"Something like that." Pablo Gomez
obviously wasn't enamored by that
interpretation of events as his superior saw
them, but as the man *was* his superior, was
unable to take against the way he'd just
interpreted things too firmly..

"Well….." Beamish began to say more but
was interrupted before he could by the others
snort of complete and utter disbelief at what he
was hearing.

. "She's a friend in need that's all." Pablo
Gomez insisted forlornly, but was interrupted
in his turn.

"How did you come to meet this woman
who must be a bad judge of character at the
very least, even if she hasn't got actual criminal
tendencies of her own?" Superintendent
Beamish was the one who was doing the
interrupting this time.

"We were at police college together a lot of
years ago." Inspector Gomez began to explain
but was interrupted before he got very far with
that explanation.

"Hmmm….." The one word reply coupled
with the look her boss had given her spoke
volumes about his disapproval of the entire
affair as he saw it.

"She's just a friend from college days whose fallen on bad times, who I tried to help out by seeing if you'd be amenable to her joining your team." Gomez tried again to put his case for including his friend in things but was interrupted once again before he could very far with that explanation by another snort of disbelief.

"My team!" Superintendant Beamish exclaimed, but whether because he doubted the veracity of the term, my team, or something else, wasn't clear.

"I'm sure she had no idea what Jones's cousin was getting up to…" Inspector Gomez began a defence of his friend, but was interrupted again.

"Just an innocent abroad I'm meant to believe am I?" Superintendant Beamish had overdone snorts of disbelief by then I felt, but he obviously didn't feel so himself, because he snorted again.

"Something like that." Inspector Gomez gave up on trying to convince the other man.

"So you want Sergeant Phyllis Fernackerly to join up with us to spike the Widow Evan's guns over the matter of female representation on my team?" Beamish sought clarity.

"I do." Pablo Gomez agreed with his chiefs assessment of things on this point at least, if not on some others it seemed..

"How do you know she'll be on our side in all this and not go siding with the Widow

Evans?" I decided that it was time for me to get involved in this and not just be an observer.

"I don't." Pablo admitted to us with a sigh.

"And you do know whether or not her tastes in life are heterosexual rather than homosexual do you?" I asked my friend Pablo a very leading question he bridled at a little.

"I don't know what it is you're suggesting in a roundabout way, but if you're asking if I've slept with her to get her to agree to this gig, I certainly haven't done anything of the sort!" Pablo Gomez insisted to us all.

"Quite the knight in shining armour aren't you?" His boss mocked him for the stance he'd taken in all this.

"I try to be if I can." Pablo Gomez said heavily.

"The point in all this though is that you agree we need female representation on our team?" I got in my oar at point to ensure where we were headed with all this.

"I do." Beamish agreed. "And at your suggestion," he nodded towards Pablo, " I agree Phyllis Fernakerly should be the one given the opportunity to become that representation. If it doesn't work out we'll have lost nothing and if it does we'll have an extra member of the team to call on."

"What are you going to do to get her?" I asked the other two interestedly.

"I thought I'd go to where she's working at present, observe her for a while to see how she performs in her present role then bring her back

116

here to have a word with you if that's alright with you?"

"Sounds perfect." Was that reply more than a little tongue in cheek I wondered.

"I'd better get to it then. She's working with Meryoneth Jones in the hotel where his cousin works at present."

"Tell you what, why not take Mark here along with you as an unbiased observer?" Beamish suggested.

"You're saying I'm not unbiased are you Superintendent?" Inspector Gomez said as if he' d expected something of the sort and wasn't phased by it.

"I'm saying you're not unbiased." Superintendent Beamish assured his underling.

CHAPTER SIXTEEN

So, at the instigation of Superintendent Beamish, I went along with Inspector Gomez to sample afternoon tea at Hilltop Hotel and observe the two police officers, one of whom might be involved in criminal activity, of some sort, as they went about their business.

Whether he had told his friend Phyllis Fernackerly we were going to be there observing her in action with her senior officer, I never found out at all.

The two police officers had slipped into the hotel unannounced in a quest to winkle out the criminals higher authority had told them might have crept in unnoticed and who must therefore be flushed out from amongst the honest patrons of the hotel.

The senior of the two officers, Meryoneth Jones claimed to have been an inspector in the special crimes unit working out of Carnarvon with special responsibilities, because of his family connections, for apprehending Welsh speaking criminals, when he applied for and got the job at the local station.

Whether he actually was what he'd claimed to be to get him there had never been out to the test. If it had been he would probably have been found to be lacking in many ways, being able to speak Welsh being one of them.

I had been told that he and his cousin, Blodwyn Cadwallader, the receptionist at Hilltop Hotel came from a criminal clan being pursued by the police of many counties and of many countries as well.

"Excuse me madam have you seen this man goes by the name of…" Meryoneth Jones was interrupting the afternoon peace and quiet of the guests who'd chosen to remain in the hotels precincts, rather than brave the fleshpots of nearby Oswestry by attempting to show them photographs he said he'd been given to him by Higher Authority. Which might or might not have been the case of course.

"Actually we don't know what name he goes by now," Meryoneth admitted after a moments thought. "Higher Authority believes he may have changed it for something else out of necessity," he showed the guest he had homed in on a picture. "This is a photo of the two toe rags we're looking for! "Have you seen them?"

After whatever the answer he had been given was he said, "thank you for your help. Don't leave the hotel without leaving a forwarding address, we may question you further." He paused and looked behind him, but there was nobody there.

"Sergeant Fernackerly, where are you?" He called urgently into the shadows. The woman I'd been waiting for with a heightened level of interest as it was possible she might be about to join Gomez's team, who was a dark haired women of medium build, dressed in unisex clothing came into view at that point.

"Coming Inspector Jones!" Phyllis Fernackerly, sounded very weary with life in general, as she picked on another diner to harass. "Excuse me, sir, have you seen this man? "We believe he's in the area, possibly with a woman we think may be his wife, or who is pretending to be his wife."

She made a note of the answers she was getting, in the book I assumed she'd been given for that purpose. Repeating out loud what had been said as she wrote it. "Thank your help." She said to the last person she'd spoken to as she walked over to where the other half of their team was waiting for her.

"Sir can I finish now please? I must have been round most of the guests now. My feet really ache!" She sat down next to the Inspector and took her shoes off to rub her foot and by doing so revealed that she had a large hole in her sock. She didn't seem a very prepossessing specimen of womanhood to me and I really couldn't see what had induced Pancho to not only become friendly with her in his own right, but then put her name forward to the Superintendent and me as someone we might want to be working with.

"That's because you haven't yet passed through the full police physical check like I have." He told the other critically. "My feet don't ache or," he sniffed the air, "pong like yours do. What you need, Sergeant Fernackerly, is more practice on the beat, then you'd be as fit as I am wouldn't you."

"Right now I know exactly what I'd like to beat," Sergeant Fernackerly studied her superior officer critically.

I could sense her contemplating whether or not she could get away with beating him to death with her shoe if she cited justifiable homicide as the grounds for taking that extreme action against him.

"Remember the anger management courses you've been on Sergeant!" Meryoneth Jones didn't appreciate just how close he was at that moment to being the recipient of that decisive response from his underling to the suggestion he'd just made to her. "I shouldn't like to have to send you back to them again." He told her. "Now breath, refocus and report your days findings so far to me."

"Not much to report yet Sir." Phyllis Fernackerly reported. Reading through her notes as she did so to ensure accuracy. "The people at table four think the photo I showed them looked vaguely familiar, but wouldn't like to say for sure.

Table five wanted me to arrest the folk on table three on suspicion of foul play. The folk on table seven requested the folk on table five be locked up indefinitely!"

"That's village politics," Inspector Jones told her sagely, "behind the rose covered front doors and "Good morning, lovely day' they're a cut throat bunch. I'd bet that there's more dangerous weapons a head in this village than in an episode of Midsummer Murders. Shot guns under the bed, cleavers in the kitchen, scythes in the barns, funny plants in the attic. They're a dangerous bunch! Keep your eye on them Sergeant Fernackerly.

"Pancho!...I mean Inspector," the woman, who became aware of my presence there as well as the other police officers, exclaimed in surprise at seeing him there, "what can I do for you?"

"What have you already been doing for him?" The unworthy thought crossed my mind as I witnessed their meeting. A meeting of lovers perhaps? I couldn't be sure. In any case, as long as she carried out the role he gave her to do, if he did, it was no business of mine what their relationship had been before our futures were linked in the way they had been.

"We have in mind for you to take over the role of investigative officer with my team if you will….." Pancho Gomez began to explain, but was interrupted. "…..We?" Her eyes moved momentarily to me, before rejecting me as possible owner of that epithet and I was quite relieved about that.

"Superintendent Beamish is my superior officer, you may know him he's based at this station?" She nodded confirmation of that knowledge on her part. "He said we needed a female officer to become part of our team…."

"Team?" She questioned sharply, but got no further before events overtook her.

"I suggested you" Gomez ignored her question, "and he agreed subject to us ironing out any problems which may arise from you partnering Meryoneth Jones for a number of years."

"Problems?" She glared at the man who might, or might not be, her some time lover, icily, daring him to enlarge on that relationship. "Perhaps you could come into my office now, and we can iron out any difficulties there may be in finalizing this, and come to an agreement over terms more easily."

Without me overhearing the fine detail, I thought a little jaundicedly, but left them both to it to sort out their rules of play, whist I got on with some parish clerk duties for one of my councils.

CHAPTER SEVENTEEN

The grandly named Western Division
Police Headquarters, where Inspector Gomez
and Superintendent Beamish first and now
Sergeant Fernackerly too, and where I had gone
by invitation to meet them and bring the
investigation involving the two women we
believed had murdered their husbands to a
conclusion, lay in the heart of Carnarvon just
off the B4366.

Carnarvon was a long way away from
Mooreland Parish and equally far away from
Beazley Parish. Not in the same county, nor in
the same country even, but it was where
Inspector Gomez and Superintendent Beamish
and now Sergeant Fernackerly too had based
themselves of late, so it was where folk
working under their auspices had to take
themselves as well.

It was also where criminals who had been
taken there on their instructions could be
processed more easily than anywhere else it
seemed to me.

One at least of the widows of the man the
police officers had had exhumed seemed most
likely to have murdered him, now it had been
proved to have been murder, but as each of
them when questioned, had said it was the other
one, her lover who did for the pair of them, it
had fallen to the police to decide where the
truth lay and which of the women should be

124

prosecuted for the crimes. Possibly both of them if they were in it together.

"She's a sister at the hospital and would certainly have the opportunities to get drugs which would kill a man and either administer them herself or get an underling to administer them for her." She reported information to the team, all of which I at least already knew, having been part of things from the beginning.

"She'll get several years for her efforts if we can prove it was her did it." Inspector Gomez considered what he hoped the probable outcome of the business was going to be for the women.

"She'll likely deny she did it when we tell her her friend said it was her." I pointed out the most likely outcome as I saw it to the brains assembled there to judge the women, and I was only too right in that assumption as it turned out.

Phyllis Fernackerly had been brought into things, according to Pablo Gomez anyway, so the investigative team wouldn't appear to be overloaded with men as it was currently.

I suspected an extra agenda on the part of the police inspector, however, who I knew from long ago, involving him getting her into bed with him at some stage in the proceedings.

Phyllis Fernnackerly, who I disapproved of for various reasons, not least her previous involvement with Merioneth Jones a policeman so bent he made the most hardened criminals seem honest by comparison.

125

She, by personal observation on my part had a notebook she carried around with her in which she jotted down things from time to time she would wish to remember for future use.

She had the notebook to hand now and was referring to it as she went, checking up on with what she was doing.

I watched her jaundicedly, wishing I had some of the power Chief Inspector Macdonald had always seemed to have had to bring matter to the conclusion he wanted it to have, humming a little ditty to herself as she went it seemed to me as I watched..

I had to admit to myself, however, that that might not have served the cause of justice as well as it did the Chief Inspectors aims, in the days when I was under his control. Then it had often seemed to me that Macdonald cared more about what the outcome of it all was than the means he'd employed to get himself there, wherever it was.

"You've got the wrong guy, Chief Superintendent." I'd protested at least once. "I don't know anything about Harry that you'd want to know, and if I did I doubt that I'd be talking about it to you. I don't go in for law-breaking myself, but I don't interfere if other people do."

"You will." Macdonald treated my words as if that was all they were - just words without any meaning to them. "Just do as I say and you will. You're a decent young fellow at heart. You've just got yourself into something you'd have done better to avoid. You'll no want to stay mixed up in it when you find out what I know about Harry."

He'd seemed so sure about what he was saying that suddenly I found myself wondering, and like a giant jigsaw in my brain pieces began to fit tentatively together.

Caroline Meredith and her father were the first pieces suddenly fitting together as if they belonged, Farrell taking a rain check on a beating and sending me on as substitute were the next.

Then Crazy Bernie first working me over in mistake for Farrell and then turning up at Harry's place. Followed by Harry warning me I'd do better to forget the whole thing.

Luella Monteith's crack about Meredith's criminal contacts, and the fact that no one would talk about the way Harry made his bread were the final pieced I had to slot in together somewhere.

There were still plenty of pieces missing yet, like what it was all about, and who were the good guys and who were the bad guys, but even I could see that there might be a connection in there somewhere if I could find it.

One thing was clear to me. Whatever it was all about, I was somewhere in the middle, and the middle wasn't a nice place to be. I looked away from the eyes that were boring into mine. "Can I go now?"

"What, here?" Macdonald had said at that point, surprised I was wanting to break free of him it seemed. "I'll take you home, laddie. It's a door to door service I'm running, ye ken."

"I'll find my own way!" Suddenly I wanted to get away from him. I needed time to think. To find the missing pieces of the jigsaw and try to fit them into place if I could.

He shrugged his shoulders. "I'll no prevent you from getting out. I've said all I was wanting to say to you. It's up to you now, and you'll be wanting this." He thrust a small card deep into the pocket of my jacket. "You'll find my telephone number on it when you need it."

"I shan't need it." I felt pretty sure on that point Complacently sure some might have said..

"You will laddie," Macdonald sounded even surer, "and just you remember one more thing." I was out of the car now and looking back in the window at him as I moved.. "You're mixed up in something big. The way I read it is it's no all your fault, but you canna escape it. Now I've offered you a way out because I'm feeling sorry for you, but I no want you getting the idea I'm soft. Help me and you're safe, whatever happens. Cross me, and I'll no be answering for the consequences. Now you remember that!"

I'd watched his car until it was out of sight and then turned and walked away in the opposite direction, my self-confidence sagging at an all-time low it had to be said.

CHAPTER EIGHTEEN

"Of course it wasn't me." Sister Evans, the nurse in black from my incarceration at the hospital, almost chewed off the end of the walking stick she'd been carrying to hand on to a patient and spat the pieces of sawdust she'd created by her action out in anger as she snarled at my presumption in being there at all I assumed, "I'm in the business of saving lives remember, something you seem to have conveniently forgotten, not ending them prematurely!"

"Despite what your friend says?" Obviously intent on having all the input she could now that she'd been allowed to take part in our investigation, Phyllis Fernackerly's words sounded almost mild by comparison I thought.

"Of course despite what my friend said!" Sister Evans glared at us all at once as she said it, not an easy feat that it had to be said as we weren't standing that close to one another.

"If she did actually say it of course," she continued to glare at us all at once. "And knowing Jay as I do, I have my doubts that she did. I think you may well have made the whole thing up for some nefarious reason of your own!"

Superintendant Beamish had taken over the running of things from our newest member, probably thinking, as I did, that that newest member might just be there as a result of sexual desire on the part of Pablo Gomez, not for the

129

investigative skills he told us we'd be getting by bringing her into the investigation.

"As a result of what your accomplice told us," the Superintendant said, "we're planning to remand you whilst we investigate those murders and any part you played in them further."

"Remand me in custody you mean?" Sister Louella Evans looked for the dotting of her is and the crossing of her tees in the answer to that question.

"Unless somebody pays your bail, of course." Phyllis Fernackerly said matter of factly as if she didn't expect that unlikely event to happen in her lifetime.

"And what did the court decide to set the bail figure at?" Sister Louella Evans, who didn't actually know the answer to her question asked us interestedly.

"The court has set your bail at ten thousand pounds sterling hasn't it?" Superintendant Beamish, who *did* know the answer to it, replied to her question.

"That's ridiculous!" Louella Evans declare angrily in response to that. "You must know that I haven't got enough money in my bank account to pay that much!"

"Find someone else who is able and prepared to pay it then!" Superintendent Beamish told her. "Meanwhile you will be remanded at a woman's prison somewhere whilst we investigate you further."

CHAPTER EIGHTEEN

Thinking back over the trail of events later, I could see that for most of the people involved they had begun when the post covid restrictions we'd all endured for a while had finally been relaxed enough for itinerent parish clerks like me to return to our face to face occupations which, in my case, might include certain procedures being carried out on our knees.

I'd chosen to have mine carried out at St Bartholomews hospital, and it had been there, the day following the operation, that the woman in the black uniform worn by senior nurses at that hospital who I thought might be a sister or something, looked at me in the disbelief that I should be there addressing her at all, having bearded her, if that was the right word to use when dealing with a woman, in her den, and then had spoken to her in a way she probably found lacking in respect for her position in the hospital, whatever that was.

Wanting to find out more about the fate of the man who'd brought round a selection books for people who couldn't get out of their beds for whatever reason, to choose from and who had brought a selection of books to me the day before and then had disappeared without trace, I'd got up early and gone deliberately to the desk where I noticed that the nurses seemed to hang out and chat to each other but there was no one at it at that moment.

I looked into the office which lay behind it and which had some sort of office title emblazoned on the front of it but was devoid of occupants at that time, then stepped cautiously into the room to address the nurse I'd seen in there. A woman dressed entirely in black it seemed to me just then.

"I was looking for the man who brings a selection of library books round every day to patients who are unable to get out of their beds themselves to choose from." I asked the only occupant of the room as far as I could see brightly.

"Why" The woman I had addressed as brightly as I could, having found her to be the only occupant of that room. asked sharply, glaring at me angrily, for my temerity in being the in the first place I assumed, as she did so.

"Why am I looking for him?" I asked a question I would have thought the answer to would have been obvious as the nurse in black continued to glare at me fiercely. Perhaps she always glared at men who had disturbed her in that ay I surmised. Perhaps no other man had ever ventured so far as to do so.

"Yes, why are you looking for him" she demanded as I paused before answering her question after a moment or two to regroup myself and decide what my answer was going to be.

"Why shouldn't I be looking for him?" I questioned the nurse in black on a point of order, feeling that as a patient, a paying patient at that. I had the right to ask whatever question I chose to ask. As long as that asking didn't take me beyond the bounds of propriety and what I had just asked the nurse surely didn't.

"Because it isn't usual for patients to get involved like that in things which don't really concern them." The nurse in black obviously saw my duties as a patient entirely different from the way in which I saw them it seemed.

She replied with the sigh of someone being put upon in a big way by having me as a patient..

"You think not?" I questioned her take on things after that lingering sigh she'd given me coupled with the look of someone being put upon even more.

"I think not." She replied. "So why are you asking me about this man and expecting me to have a suitable reply on hand?"

"Because he told me there were two men he knew of who'd died in this hospital without good cause since he'd been coming here handing out books for patients to read?" I replied simply. Telling her no more than the truth as I saw it.

"Because he told you there were two men he knew of who'd died in this hospital without good cause since he'd been coming here handing out books for patients to read?" She repeated to me what I'd just told her, in tones of complete and utter disbelief.

"He did, sister." I assumed in my reply that that must be the rank of the woman I was facing, well aware that my words weren't being well received by her.

I could hardly be surprised that they weren't because, even if not true she would have still seen it as a slur on her hospital. Not surprising under the circumstances

"What were the names of these two men who died in our hospital though they shouldn't have done according to you?" She glared back at me, asking what, under the circumstances probably seemed a very pertinent question to her.

CHAPTER NINETEEN

"What were the names of these two men who died in our hospital though they shouldn't have done according to you?" The nurse in black demanded of me, Glaring She glared back at me, as she did so for asking what, under the circumstances probably seemed a very pertinent question to her.

Pertinent to me also I had to admit silently to myself without giving that fact away in my reply because I wasn't able to. "He didn't tell me that I'm afraid," our conversation not having progressed that far at the time, I thought, but didn't say so, of disclosing the names of his alleged murder victims to me.

"When were they actually here as patients?" The nurse in black asked another leading question of me. One which again I couldn't answer as it happened, because my thinking it over hadn't got to that point at the time.

"He didn't tell me that either." I had to concede reluctantly. Very reluctantly it had to be said. Because he hadn't, our conversation not having progressed that far, and now never would, of course, circumstances having overtaken us all.

"Didn't tell you, Mr Montgomery!" The nurse swelled visibly at that in complete disbelief, probably that I should have set this thing in motion without knowing that, at least.

"And then he died immediately afterwards in what seemed very suspicious circumstances to me." I pointed out pertinently. "Falling down several flights of stairs after being pushed by some interested party to start him on his way perhaps!"

My previous experience with murders and murderers thanks to Chief Inspector Macdonald, making my mind turn to that line of thought more quickly than it might otherwise have done with most patients she'd had to encounter, probably.

"What do you say they had wrong with them, these patients who died under mysterious circumstances, that they shouldn't have died of?" The nurse in black demanded of me.

"He didn't tell me that either." I had to admit reluctantly again, because he hadn't, our conversation asked me what to her must have seemed an obvious question to be asking not having progressed that far at the time. And now never would of course, given the circumstances, I thought pertinently again.

"Do you think he might have just been trying to compete with the story you'd just told him," the nurse in the black uniform, who may or may not have been the sister at that hospital, asked what also probably seemed an obvious question to her. "In my experience of men they do that sort of thing a great deal don't they? Trying to be top dog in all walks of life."

"Do they?" I genuinely had no idea at all where the woman was going with that line of thought. "What sort of things do you mean?" I asked with no idea at all of where this was taking us.

"Compete with each other over inconsequential things." She said simply. Speaking as if to a mentally retarded patient. Looking me up and as appraisingly as she said it as the as the ward orderly before had done. It's the alpha male syndrome taken to extremes. Why did he tell you about this supposed patient in the first place?"

"I'd just told him how someone had tried to kill me when they thought I'd seen them murdering someone else. Even though I hadn't really."

"And he wanted to be the one to slash highest up the wall than you had?" She summed me up to her own satisfaction, as she declared with venom.

"Is that what you mean by that?" I suddenly grasped what she'd been leading towards with her questioning and didn't like the line she was taking at all.

"Something like that, Mr Montgomery, something like that." She agreed with me with a smile I found irritating in the extreme, though I tried to hide the fact. Probably not very successfully that maneouvre I have to say.

"So you won't investigate the story he told me then?" I got straight to the point she'd been trying to make to me without preamble or social niceties.

"I've got too many other things to do!" She told me caustically. "More important things by

far! I haven't time to waste time over
something which more than likely didn't
happen in the first place!" She told me
caustically.

"I should think you'll get on better with
your investigation, if you intend carrying on
with it, once you get back home amongst
familiar people and things." Another nurse had
joined the other one now, this one not in black
though, but in the normal uniform most nurses
were wearing. She stood close to the first one
as if to express solidarity with her in the face of
a stroppy patient, namely me.

CHAPTER TWENTY

"What do you mean I can carry on my investigation at home? You're saying I'm going home then?" I was news to me if I was. As far as I'd noticed no one had got out of the place so swiftly before. In fact most folk seemed to be held back in the place long after they wanted to be free of it and couldn't wait to get away.

"You're going home." The lower echelon nurse confirmed what the one I took to be her superior had said. "I've just been clearing your bed of your belongings in readiness for that to happen! Without hindrance from you"

"But I'm not going home until the doctor tells me I'm being discharged and he didn't do that when he did his round this morning I promise you. Didn't even look at me as far as I recall!" I reported what had happened to me.

"You're going home." The lower echelon nurse confirmed her superiors take on things. "You'll find your bed has been cleared to make way for a new patient."

"Yes, you're leaving us, I've been told." The woman in black had returned to confirm the fact. "And that's why your clothes have been moved off your bed in readiness for that to happen."

"I don't think so." I disagreed with that summing up of things. Deciding to stand up for my rights as a patient, as I saw it. "I'm not due to go until the consultant declares me fit.

139

I'm not allowed to leave until the consultant I saw declares me fit enough to do so. It says so in your manifesto! You should read it some time."

"That's all gone by the board I'm afraid." The nurse in black, a tall woman, deliberately moved closer to tower over me threateningly, as she told me authoritatively. "We need your bed for someone else."

"Who?" I enquired sharply. Not believing that story for a moment. Suspecting something more sinister than my bed being needed for another patient was behind my unheralded departure.

"For am an emergency who has just been brought in." The nurse in black, still towering above me, said sharply and so, despite my protests whin I knew from the first were going to be in vain, my stay at St Bartholomews ended ignominiously.

"Why did you have to interfere and not leave well alone?" I'd woken to the strident ringing of the telephone on my bedside table, which, when I'd lifted the receiver to find out who was there, had turned out to be the voice of the nurse in black, the Sister my colleagues and I, on the authority of her friend and sometime partner Jay Lane, believed was to have been responsible for the deaths of at least three men as a direct result of that questionable relationship.

I was glad that she was only on the end of a phone line, not close enough to me to do what the Black Widow, the Russian assassin I'd encountered before, could have done to me if she'd chosen to.

The widow I was involved with now, not a spider but a real life woman in human form, was a different kettle of fish entirely.

The Widow Evans, who, luckily for me was on the end of a phone line I felt would do all that the Russian assassin could have done and more if only I was close enough to her to do it, just for the hell of being able to do it to me too.

"Why does anyone choose to interfere and not leave well alone?" I asked what was only intended to be a rhetorical question anyway, but I felt that the Widow Evans wasn't really interested in what I had to say in any case, just gratified that she had the opportunity to disturb my sleep in the manner that she had.

"It was only because we were both women that that hateful man put his oar in the first place." She carried on, sounding bitter at the memory. "Saw us together once, being friendlier than we should have been in public I suppose, touching hands or kissing or something. I really don't really remember now. After that he wouldn't let it go!"

"Oh." I assumed the Widow Evans hadn't really wanted a verbal response from me when she'd made her phone call early enough to disturb my sleep, but I gave her one anyway.

"Colin Croft you mean? He didn't seem a hateful person to me, just someone I found useful when I was in bed unable to move and

141

he was doing the library run in the hospital. I
didn't have your particular foible to upset him
with though I suppose."

CHAPTER TWENTY ONE

"Why did you have to interfere and not leave well alone?" I'd woken to the strident ringing of the telephone on my bedside table, which, when I'd lifted the receiver to find out who was there, had turned out to be the voice of the nurse in black, the Sister my colleagues and I, on the authority of her friend and sometime partner Jay Lane, believed was to have been responsible for the deaths of at least three men as a direct result of that questionable relationship.

I was glad that she was only on the end of a phone line, not close enough to me to do what the Black Widow, the Russian assassin I'd encountered before, could have done to me if she'd chosen to do so to me.

The widow I was involved with now wasn't a spider, or any form of insect, not a spider but a real life woman in human form, was a different kettle of fish entirely.

The Widow Evans, who, luckily for me was on the end of a phone line I felt would do all that the Russian assassin could have done and more if only I was close enough to her to do it, just for the hell of being able to do it to me too.

"Why does anyone choose to interfere and not leave well alone?" I asked what was only intended to be a rhetorical question anyway, but I felt that the Widow Evans wasn't really interested in what I had to say in any case, just gratified that she had the opportunity to disturb my sleep in the manner that she had.

"It was only because we were both women that that hateful man put his oar in the first place." She carried on, sounding bitter at the memory. "Saw us together once, being friendlier than we should have been in public I suppose, touching hands or kissing or something. I really don't really remember now. After that he wouldn't let it go the dreadful fellow!"

"Oh." I assumed the Widow Evans hadn't really wanted any sort of verbal response from me when she'd made her phone call early enough to disturb my sleep, but I had given her one anyway.

"Colin Croft you mean? He didn't seem a hateful person to me, just someone I found useful when I was in bed unable to move and he was doing the library run in the hospital. I didn't have your particular foible to upset him with though I suppose."

"It began with the Covid outbreak," She said ruminatively, not picking up at all on what I'd said about believing Colin Croft to have been a good guy with a useful purpose in life, "a time when, after the total lockdown had ended, folk were able to share shopping on line if they chose to." She sighed at the memory.

"It became very clear very quickly to the people involved that two of us who had chosen to do so, Jay and I, simply weren't compatible where online shopping was concerned.

Not our fault I guess, we'd only been thrown together initially by the covid lockdown, without which neither would have become that closely involved with each other. Even though we saw each other most days at work, that relationship was carried on on a different kind of footing entirely. ….."

The Widow Evan's voice tailed off as she seemed to be reliving those times in her mind, and I was about to make some sort of suitable reply just to keep the conversation going, when she carried on ruminatively once again, not needing that prompt at all.

"Payment for our shared shopping seemed to be what irritated my friend and lover Jay the most with my constant questions about it, she said.

"Not nearly as much as Jay soon drove me to distraction, however, with her demands for more information that I was able to give her at the time. It was obvious the two of us shouldn't have tried doing anything together, never mind on line shopping in which it alternated month by month which of us was responsible for choosing what we were buying and which of us was responsible for paying for it.

It ended up with us hating each other passionately because of our shared endeavours, and yet at the same time in a strange way, I found myself having feelings about her I simply shouldn't have had. Not both of us being women as we were……"

Her voice tailed off again and again I considered making some sort of comment to fill the awkward silence which had fallen between us but felt there wasn't really any comment I could make which wouldn't have sounded crass in the extreme.

Besides, Widow Evans as I called her in my mind because of my earlier association with the hired assassin of similar name I'd known before, who, as I recalled, had been telling me like it was, not inviting comment from me that day in the bower in my garden.

She might well have been following the same formula as the Black Widow because she continued in the same reflective tone of voice. "The need for the pair of us to get into bed together like a couple ought to and have a sexual encounter of some sort had become paramount in my mind at least, if not in Jays, just as the Covid outbreak began to show signs of coming to an end.

I found myself wondering to myself what Jay would do if I made a move on her to get her into bed with me. How she would respond to any approach of that kind.

Although we were both married women with husbands, or with a partner in Jay's case, at least, because of that dangerous attraction Jay was generating towards me, without apparently realising she was doing it, I found myself needing to have sex in some form with her, whilst day dreaming about the possibility of bringing that growing need in me to fruition.

When the Covid outbreak and supermarket shopping together finally seemed to be coming to an end and I was able to avoid direct contact with Jay I was initially relieved.

Even though we still saw each other at work, it was a distant relationship which allowed me to keep my feelings for Jay hidden. Despite that though, I still couldn't get rid of the need I felt to enjoy Jay's body to the full, at least once, whatever that meant for the two of us, and see where, if anywhere, that took us.

I had no way of knowing whether or not Jay shared the feelings which dominated my life at that moment, assuming that, as another woman she would be shocked and disgusted if I revealed them to her so I took care to avoid doing that.

Life after Covid was gradually returning to normal, villagers were able to visit other villagers if they chose to. That was how I came upon Jay walking through her village on her way home after being let down by the woman in the village she had intended having afternoon tea with.

I admit I had sometimes driven through Jay's village on my day off without really knowing why, usually without seeing her at all. This time though I did see her and though if common sense had prevailed, I would have just carried on driving, instead of passing her by with no more than a casual wave, as I should have done if common sense had prevailed, I found myself stopping alongside her and

147

offering her a lift to her home if she wanted one.

Having noted who it was hailing her as someone she knew well enough to get into a car beside her, Jay, who I usually only saw in the hospital scrubs she wore at work but who, on this occasion, as a result of going to visit a friend at the other end of her village, who had been out when she called, was wearing a flowery summers dress for the occasion, got into the back of the car instead of the front of it when I explained there was something on the front passenger seat I didn't want folk sitting on and damaging in some way.

That was a make or break moment for me, I know, because I could still have taken Jay where I was supposed to have taken her, back to her home, instead, acting entirely on impulse, I drove to a discreet corner of the local woods, parked carefully, taking care to remove the key from the ignition, got into the back of the car beside Jay and found myself doing the things to her I had day dreamed of doing so many times, but which I had feared the opportunity to do now had passed,.

I kissed her purposefully, using my tongue with gay abandon, whilst I slipped my hand up under the hem of the flowery dress, which I have to admit I had found very inviting, I sniffed the scanty briefs which were all she was wearing under it thoughtfully, then chewing them equally thoughtfully, before fixing them to the top of my head, wearing them like a crown of triumph for all I felt she had achieved already, as things seemed to be panning out the way I had hoped, but never, in my wildest dreams, really believed they would.

My fingers, meanwhile were plunging ever deeper into Jays vagina, whilst my mouth, freed from duties chewing Jays underwear, was concentrating on her clitoris sucking it with abandon whilst her tongue performed sterling services of exploration too, hoping I might be raising Jay to new paroxysms of delight as I transferred its activity to Jays clitoris, sucking and licking it purposefully……I don't suppose you even know what that is?"

The Widow Evans took a moment to comment on what she obviously considered to be my lack of knowledge on the subject. "Most men don't have any idea at all!" She commented to me caustically.

"I… I…" I managed to mutter before the voice on the phone overrode any reply I might have been intending to make about my lack of, or fully operational knowledge on the subject, of women's bodies. "Do we have to go on with this?" I managed to stutter out the question at last, because I was feeling more than a little overwhelmed by her account of her seduction of the other suspect in three murders, exciting as it all may have been for her at the time I assumed.

"Yes you do!" The Widow Evans replied sharply. Not giving me a moment's quarter it seemed. "You asked to get involved in this, and now you're obliged to hear me through to the bitter end!"

"No I'm not!" I disputed sharply. Not having any memory of signing on for such an explicit account of lesbian sex. " I didn't ask you to phone me in the dead of night and reveal all in that way."

"Put the phone down then. If you're so disgusted by my story!" She advised me, but I knew that I couldn't. Having heard so much of it now I would have to follow her story through to the bitter end, if only to be able to repeat to the two police officers what she'd said to me.

She knew that as well as I did that that was going to be the case for me for whatever reason I chose to excuse it with because she carried on with her story without actually making sure I was listening to it.

"Jay's only response to all this frenzied activity on my part had been to grip the cushion of the seat she was sitting on and swearing a couple of times.

Fearing this might be my only chance of making love to her like that, before she stopped me in disgust," the voice on the end of the phone line, that of the nurse in black, the sister from St Gregorys hospital, or the Widow Evans I assumed, continued recounting what had brought them both to that, and three men, so far, to their deaths, "and I'd have to live on the memory of that moment of fulfilment for the rest of my life, I did all the things to Jay I'd been dreaming of doing to her if I ever got the chance and then some I made up as I went along, borrowing heavily on woman to woman porn I 'd found on the internet one time.

Eventually I stopped what I was doing, immediate needs sated, and, deliberately sitting back on the seat away from Jay, looked into her eyes for a moment or two, trying to gauge whether or not Jay was about to express disgust at being taken advantage like that by another woman who was also a neighbour.

"I'm sorry, Jay if it seemed to you I was taking advantage of you doing what I was doing," I said at last when Jay didn't make any comment at all, "it wasn't like that at all. I've been needing to make love to you like that since you used since you used to wind me up so badly over the shared shopping we did during covid and had to be content with the regular tongue lashings I had to give Eddie instead out of sheer frustration.......

"What?" The Widow Evans asked as I made a noise in my throat suggestive of having had enough of this story of hers she might have been seeing as romantic, but I was like the man who'd fallen to his death in the hospital, sated by so much perversion.

"You can't possibly know how much I'd needed to what I've just done I told Jay," Widow Evans continued, "however distasteful it might seem to everyone else, even to you yourself, Jay, whilst I was doing it. I'd needed to have you like that, badly needed it I have to say, and was afraid if I stopped you wouldn't let me do it again. Whether you believe me or not, I'd had to have her like that at least once in my life if never again......"

Jay stopped me at that point with a smile. "You *were* taking advantage of me Lou she said. There's no getting around that fact! Whatever flowery terms you couched it in. Forcing yourself on me on the back seat of your car like that, like you were a man and I was just your strumpet, when I'd expected to be taken home as promised by a woman I saw as a friend. I wasn't used to being treated like that by anyone in my life, least of all another woman!...

What?" Widow Evans demanded as I, in the persona of Mark Montgomery, parish clerk now, interrupted her, having recognised the story the two police officers and I been told by Jay Lane. Was it only the day before?

"So you *did* take advantage of her then! It wasn't all sweetness and romantic suppers between the two of you?" I would have expected nothing else from the woman who'd seemed intent in getting her own way at every turn when I was within her compass incarcerated in the hospital.

"No I hadn't take advantage of her as it turned out," The Widow Evans disputed my take on things, "Jay told me she'd been wanting, no needing, to get inside my knickers since we shared that internet shopping during the covid lockdown and I used to drive her mad with my impossible demands .... just as much as I had obviously wanted to get inside hers, but had no idea what do next until I showed the way.

That being the case she intended doing all the things back to me I'd just been doing to her if I helped her at first, despite never having had sex with another woman before!..... What do you want now?" She demanded as I made a noise suggestive of me interrupting her once again.

Mostly because I couldn't take much more of her story it had to be said. Especially as it had ended with three men dying because of it, either at her hands or the other woman's, or the two of them in partnership with each other. Something she seemed to be totally overlooking in all this. Perhaps because all the victims had been men and therefore, in her eyes al least, expendable.....

"How long we were actually there enjoying each others bodies learning about each others needs neither of us really knew," Widow Evans continued, "but after leaning against each other in companionable for it while it seemed right to go back to real life and away from all this passion, unless....

"Perhaps next time we ought to try someone's bed," Jay suggested, "mine perhaps. It would be considerably more comfortable than this car of yours has been."

"Next time?" Lou questioned.

"There's going to be one I assume," Jay commented, "If we organise it right there wouldn't be any need for anyone ese, our husbands for instance, to find out wouldn't you say Lou?"

"So that was what you did. For a while at least but unfortunately one of you had more in mind in not involving your husbands than the other did and that resulted in repercussions for the two of you neither had expected." In Mark the Clerk mode again, I pointed out to the voice on the phone.

That *was* when Colin Croft began looking at how our husbands died in the first place". Widow Evans agreed. "I can tell you now that he was right about that. I made sure my husband was cremated so there's no remains of him to exhume, Jays partner though, insisted on being buried so his remains are there to examine if you can manage it to get all the right licences in place.

I overheard you when you were telling him about your escapade when that former spy, the black widow, another woman who'd been mistreated by men all her life and tried to kill you as a result tied to kill you, and I thought he's going to have to top that story in some way and the only way he can top it is telling you about us I knew he was intending to tell you about Jay and me and our husbands as a means of surpassing what you'd told him.

It was a spur of the moment thing really seeing him standing where he was right on the edge of the stairs. No one there to see what I was doing when I did it so I gave him a hefty

154

shove which sent him careering down the stairs to his death. Though I didn't know that'd be that outcome when I pushed him I wasn't sorry when he died." Widow Evans finished her story.

CHAPTER TWENTY TWO

It was a day or two later when my zoom camera beeped at me uncertainly and I picked it up from my desk where it had been laying at rest, just awaiting the chance to upset the timbre of day, which had been uneventful until that moment, and I had been content for it to stay that way too, to find the familiar face of Pablo Gomez smiling at me uncertainly.

"Someone paid the bail." He announced to me without preamble, assuming from the events of the past few days it seemed, that I would know without being given any hint to start my mind heading in the right direction, just who it was he was referring to with that opening gambit of his.

"Someone paid the bill!" I repeated, not entirely disbelievingly because I had expected something of the sort to happen before this was all over and the fat lady sang. "Who the devil would do that?"

"It seems that it was her friend who did the honours in the matter." He told me as if he couldn't quite believe it either but the friend had just done so and on his watch too.

"This *is* the friend who told us it was the Widow Evans who murdered both of their husbands without her knowing anything about it any input from her when we interviewed them?" I swore in disbelief at what I was saying as I said it.

"It is. Jay Lane her name was. Reluctant to tell us the complete story as I recall." He confirmed what I'd just told him. Was going to come back the next day to do that, but never did as I recall." Pancho Gomez whistled a little at the memory of what had gone down. O hadn't gone down in this case as it turned out.

"Changed her mind I suppose and decided to plough her own furrow in this and not help her friend out at all." Superintendent Beamish pushed his way forward to the front of the camera lens to speak in the background of Pablo's zoom.

"I don't think that was what happened at all." I was able, not being connected to the two policemen at all to plough *my* own furrow in this. "I reckon, knowing she's guilty, she's going to jump bail first chance she gets to escape her just deserts!" I remarked sagely, having given the matter a lot of thought.

"What," The Superintendent questioned the veracity of my observation, however much thought on my part had gone into it. "and leave her friend to lose the money she paid for the bail?"

"And leave her friend to lose the money she paid the court." I summed up the most likely outcome of it all as I saw it.

CHAPTER TWENTY THREE

A car I had come to recognize as that belonging to Inspector Pancho Gomez made a careful entrance to my garden as I sat alone contemplating life in general and my own part in it with all its attendant failings.

"I thought I'd pay you a visit rather than zooming you again." The Inspector said as he wound down his window to address me. "Not been out in the sticks for such a long time I thought I'd have a trip out into the country this time."

"And this is so much more like being out in the country than your usual haunts are." I commented a bit sarcastically, "usually working out of Carmarthen as you do. So what are you planning to do." I asked him interestedly.

"That depends how things pan out." The inspector admitted, going on to enlarge on things a little bit unhappily it seemed to me. "They jumped bail those two women you know?" He said as if he hadn't expected or planned for such an outcome despite everything.

Not being the least bit surprised by that as a result of my midnight phone all from the Widow Evans I was able to treat the entire matter more nonchalantly than I might otherwise have done.

"Did they?" I said, not being the least bit surprised by that revelation of course. "Oh!"

"That Jay put up the bail money to get her friend out of prison. He went on "and then Lou jumped jail immediately." The Superintendant said as if he at least couldn't believe it.

"Jay has also disappeared I hear." The Inspector filled in the stop press news he had to deliver, "Away from home and home and family. We don't expect to see either of them again. Good riddance too!" he went on after a bit of thought on the subject.

"Off abroad somewhere I imagine," I summed the events up as I saw it.

"Probably lying out together on a quiet beach in the sunshine." Pablo Gomez summed things up as he saw them too.

"Lou did phone me in the early hours one morning to say goodbye on the telephone before they went. She said she didn't bear me a grudge for my part in things."

"That was good of her." I wasn't sure whether or not Pablo really meant what he was saying.

"Didn't try to kill you as a parting gesture like that other woman did. I expect they're laying on a sunny beach in the sunshine." He concluded his account.

"Good luck to them if they are." Pablo Gomez had obviously given matters a lot of thought over the previous twenty four hours or so he'd had to pass.

"I don't bear them any grudges wherever they are and whatever they're doing. They gave me an interest to follow during my weeks of

159

recuperation." I summed things up as I saw
them.

The End

Now you've finished this book why not read one of Brian W Taylor's other stories available both as e-books and paperbacks from Amazon.

The Lady of the Marshes - The north Norfolk coast in the autumn of 1917. A restless ghost searches for a means of experiencing physical love again. A teenage girl tries to find her way through the pitfalls of a first emotional encounter. A ruthless woman determines to hold on to her family's estates in the face of all adversity. A soldier is invalided home from the battlefields of France, suffering from amnesia. Add incest, espionage and murder, then look for the answer to the question posed on a suicide's grave. Why Weeps the Willow?

Let Sleeping Evils Lie – a midnight vigil in a churchyard by students trying to contact a ghost said to haunt it, and some impromptu dabbling with an Ouija board in a youth club a few days later, awaken a sleeping evil it would have been better to leave undisturbed.

Haunted Hearts - The team in charge of the gardens at Moorecroft Hall really believed they'd invented the idea a Grey Lady running along a haunted track, screaming for her husband to save her from the executioners axe, in order to draw in the punters on dark winter's nights. But they were wrong.

Through chance, or a conspiracy of fates, the track along which they'd set their imaginary ghost to run really had been haunted. Haunted for longer than the house had stood. Haunted by a constantly recurring cycle of love, betrayal and murder, which had already continued for centuries, and seemed likely to be repeated ad infinitum, unless someone came along to break the cycle somehow. But was that ever likely to happen after it had been going on for so long? And if so how?

Murder in the Marches – The wreckage of a millionaire's plane found crashed onto the side of a Welsh mountain. A burned out holiday cottage deep in the Welsh Marches, with the remains of a body still smouldering amongst the ashes. A mysterious package missing, first from the plane, and then from the cottage, that everyone is looking for, but no one can find. Too busy looking over their shoulders trying to see what the next guy is doing, no one is watching Chief Inspector Macdonald, but he's the one pulling the strings.

The Body in the Woods - A man slumped beside ruins in the woods, in Shropshire, whispering dying words about a destroying angel.

The body of a man lying in the cottage the first man had lived in, clutching a package to his chest someone had been prepared to kill him to get back.

If it's a quiet life you're looking for, Shropshire simply isn't a good place to retire to, not as long as Chief Inspector Macdonald is still there pulling the strings.

The Disenchanted Garden - An eighteenth century landscape garden, with lake, woodlands, statuary and buildings designed by Humphry Repton, Middleton Hall, as envisaged by its owners, and set out by its designer, was meant to be an enchanted garden in every sense of the word, but even before it was swallowed up by urban sprawl during the twentieth century, something had gone seriously wrong with that initial idea. The lives and loves of people in a suburban park in the summer of 1983, and their involvement in a tree planting ceremony to commemorate a sharp tongued local councillor's twenty five years of service.

Reluctant Time Travellers - A gang of gypsies who have crashed through the barriers of time and space to sell the people they have kidnapped in your world and dimension as slaves to labour in the fire ice mines in another one. They have been doing it successfully for more than five hundred years now. And now you've just fallen into their clutches.

How easy is it going to be to escape from them by reversing the spell which makes it possible for them to do what they do and return to your own time and dimension?

Inadvertant Time Travellers - Aurora Bradley refused to believe she was surrounded by fairies, elves, sorcerers, and a boy who'd turned himself into a talking cat as a result of a curse which went wrong, the first time she found herself in Madragora. An alternative world into which she accidently passed by way of a hidden time portal at the end of her aunt's garden, when she eventually escaped from Madragora, she had no memory of ever having been there at all. Now, after visiting her aunt again and encountering the same boy turned into a talking cat she didn't believe in before, and fleeing from him through the same time portal, she finds herself back in Madragora, with no memory of ever having been there before. So why do people she's sure she's never met before seem to know her name and believe she's there to honour a promise to one of them she doesn't remember ever making? And how, if ever, is she going to find her way back to her own world a second time?

Reluctant Time Travellers Return to Madragora

The next book in the Mark the Clerk
Murder Mysteries will be "Losing the Plot" the
first chapter or which follows

CHAPTER ONE

The Village History commissioned by
Lacey Parish Council whilst I was its clerk had
first been mooted as something the parish
should to do when the millennium loomed large
on everyone's horizon. It wasn't written and
published at the time but a year or two later.
When it was eventually written, however
researchers discovered a link between a rich
American and his family who used to live in
the village and had been paying for the upkeep
of his grave for a number of years.

Now, as incoming clerk, newly taking
over that job, and any others which stemmed
from it I had been given the job of finding out
why the famous man had no gravestone to
mark his passing before the television company
got irretrievably involved and their plan to do a
feature on the man and his family became a
reality. Starting around the grave for which the
family have been paying the upkeep of for a
number of years.

The family was said to have left
England with the Pilgrim Fathers and a pageant
was in the planning stages centring on the
grave, as a result. The only trouble with that

was that no one in the village had the slightest
idea where the grave was, the church
authorities especially.

That was why, when I was parish clerk
I had been called on to investigate and find out
where the moneys supposedly used for the
upkeep of the grave of the president elect, had
gone. Not to mention the gravestones which,
which ought to have prominent in the
graveyard but weren't.

During the early sixties I discovered
through investigation there had been a tendency
to clear graveyards for easier maintenance to
allow workers to get larger mowers into the
space provided.

It was then that many of the
gravestones were removed. Some left leaning
against the churchyard wall, some moved away
to places unknown with unrecorded destination.
Some of those belonging to local landowners
had been broken up as foundation for a variety
of building projects in the village, though
where and how they were nobody really knew.
The age of on any of the gravestones left
standing would have faded over the years
anyway and not be legible anymore.

In the beginning the church records, as
I found out during he course of my
investigations, would have been lodged with
the vicar for him or her to take care of them,
but these were eventually moved to the record

166

offices where they were mostly less easily available to people who wanted to read them.

Investigation into that aspect of recent life in the village on my part had revealed that there had been gravestones marking burials which had been cleared away to make it easier to cut the grass around the graves with the largest machine available and not only that, the gravestones which at first had been leaning tidily against the churchyard wall nearby had been taken away by a farmer who hadn't any right to do so really, to make cheap hardcore for a road he was building across his fields leading to his farmyard.

Most church records at that time were to be found in the vestry of the church, or else digitalised and moved to the county record office to be examined at leisure by those allowed to do so.

The former was what had happened to the Lacey records, which were there to be looked at by anyone prepared to pay the sun demanded for it. You had to get the keys to the vestry from whichever of the wardens was available for the purpose, find yourself somewhere to sit in the story where you could see what you were doing. Old church records were very heavy documents to heave about on your own as I had discovered through bitter personal experience.

My first move after taking over proceedings had been to get together with one or two of those interested parties who were prepared to get involved, or said they would anyway, most of those volunteers having found out how heavy the records were and how cold the vestries were losing interest very swiftly.

Nor did most of them have a lot of time to spend on the project themselves, so had drifted off to their less dusty normal lives, none of them volunteering to help me to put the heavy boxes packed with papers of use to anyone compiling a village history.

It was then that I was interrupted by a girl who hadn't been part of my original work party, but who had emerged from I knew not where, after the others drifted off to go their separate ways, none of them volunteering to help me to put anything away. It highlighted the need for a village hall where such things could be stored in some fashion I thought.

The girl who had joined my work party after most of my volunteers had thought better of their involvement and gone back to their normal lives very swiftly was small, dark, and very pretty. In appearance, no more than eighteen or nineteen years old. Dressed in a blue uniform of a dress her figure flattered. Where she'd appeared from I'd been too distracted to notice at the time.

"It's a lovely day isn't it?" She smiled at me without apparent embarrassment as I struggled with my arms full of boxes of files she made no obvious move of any sort to help me with.

I strove to keep my irritation at the intrusion from being apparent. Had I met the girl at any other time I might have responded to her looks. The clear blue of eyes a lighter shade than the uniform she wore, the red of lips half open and inviting, the wisps of escaped hair, which lay along the nape of her neck as it curved down towards her shoulders, might all have worked their magic. As it was, I simply wanted the chance to struggle back to my rooms in the pub where I could be by myself and think.

"If I hadn't the need to put all these boxes away without assistance, it probably would be," I agreed easily, looking away from her into the distance. Her proximity was even more disturbing than her presence. Sitting where she was, her ankles emerged invitingly from a froth of petticoats just on a level with my eyes if I looked in that direction which I was trying my hardest not to do.

"What are you doing? And why are you doing it" She asked interestedly, apparently not noticing the disquiet her presence was causing me. Or if she did, she didn't let it show at all.

"Trying to find out anything about the lack of gravestones in churchyard here." I said "Do you know why there aren't any to be seen?" I sighed loudly, wishing she might have chosen a different lane in which to seek out someone with whom to pass a lazy afternoon. Pretty as she was, just at that moment I could see no great attraction in her company. "I thought

169

someone would help me carry them back to where I got them from but nobody wanted to help me." I complained.

"There's no need to be so crabby about it," the girl admonished me coldly. "*I* didn't make them go away did I? What's your name by the way?" She continued regarding me interestedly

"Mark Montgomery," I answered briefly.

"Mine's Rebecca Melchin," she pulled a face. "Dreadful name! I'd much rather be called Becky, but father doesn't approve of abbreviations or nick names.

Roy used to call me Becky, but he died in an accident last year, and there was no one else to call me that once he'd gone. Will you call me Becky?" She said without apparent reason.

"If you want me to," the twists and turns of her conversation were doing nothing at all to ease my headache, "but am I likely to have much opportunity for that?" I asked her pertinently.

"If you're living at Lacey you will. My father's the vicar there." She explained with a smile.

"Don't tell him about seeing me here if you meet him though. I'm supposed to be indoors cleaning the silver for the lady I work for at the big hall at the moment, but it was too nice a day to spend cooped up inside, so I slipped out instead. I can always do the silver tonight when everyone else is in bed.

170

Father wouldn't understand that if you told him though. He'd believe I was failing in some way."

"What gave you the idea I'm living in Lacey?" I asked with a frown, not so sure I was taken with this girl who seemed too familiar by far.

"*Everybody* lives in Lacey!" She said sharply. "That's why! What makes you so different from everyone else that you wouldn't be living there?"

"You're right I suppose but I'm only working in Lacey, staying at the Black Dog pub whilst I'm doing research into a family who used to live here. Looking at gravestones to see if I can find one that's missing, going back home every night to sift through what I've found out during the day. Going back to the room I've taken at the pub to sift through my findings, because it's a bit closer than me going home. Hoping that someone other than me is going to get involved."

"But no one has as yet?" She pointed out pertinently.

"No one has as yet." I agreed unhappily.

"Not surprising is it." She pointed out a truth I'd tried to avoid facing, despite the self evident truth before me, that *most* people didn't want to get involved with what I was doing. Even her.

"If you say so." I said sadly.

"I could help if you; like." She offered half heartedly it seemed to me. "I've got nothing else I have to be doing, other than dusting and cleaning, and I hate doing that. It would be good to have an excuse to get away from it."

"Supposing someone finds out you're not doing what you're supposed to be doing?" I pointed out to her pertinently.

"You won't tell anyone will you? Tell me about this flower instead," she plucked a blossom from an entanglement of trailing stems binding the hedgerow hazels beside her, then turned back towards me, holding it in front of her like a shield.

"It's columbine, the flower of deserted lovers." I said, because it happened to be one that I knew.

"Is it?" She twisted the stem nervously around her fingers. "How do you know that that's its name?"

A good question. Why should I remember that? "Somebody must have told me," I answered briefly, "I don't remember who."

"Somebody spurned in love perhaps," a spark of interest lightened her face. Clearly the unfortunate Roy's moment was passing. "Someone who.... Do you like to read tombstones?" Her mind went off at an apparent tangent.

"When they are there to read I do." I answered abstractedly, wondering how she had come to hit on my interest in tombstones which I was pretty sure I hadn't mentioned to her, my thoughts still taken up with the Columbine.

"You should try it," she declared enthusiastically. "I read those in father's churchyard whenever I get the chance. Some of the epitaphs there are quite beautiful. The warmth of worldly love engraved on cold stone. Frozen tears, Roy called them once.

'Why weeps the willow? Why cries the rain? Still lies the lonely heart, which always beat in vain'. That's my favourite.

It's supposed to be the grave of a girl who killed herself whilst her lover was away at war. That's why it's alone in unconsecrated ground. It was outside the churchyard until they began to extend the boundary wall last month.......

"Which war was he away at?" I asked interested in a tombstone which was clearly missing.

"I don't really know, just that the story goes that when the soldier came home from the war and found out what had happened, he had the cross made and put it on her grave. He wasn't supposed to. Suicides aren't allowed crosses or anything like that, but he put it there himself just the same. No name, though, to say who she was and, according to what someone told me, the soldier was killed soon after he went back to the war.

Don't you think that's a beautiful story? Almost like something you might read in a book. I enjoy stories about star-crossed lovers, don't you? Not that I get the chance to read many of them. Father doesn't approve....." She stood up suddenly, looking past me in the direction of Lacey and interrupting herself to say. "There's a carriage coming along the lane.

173

Oh no! It's her who I work for! I must get out of sight before she sees me! Please don't give me away!" She scrambled back out of sight, all petticoats and black stockings, and in a moment I was to all intents and purposes alone.

"Why don't you flag the carriage down and ask her if she'll take you and your cases to the Black Dog, or somewhere close to it?" Becky's disembodied voice asked suddenly from her hiding place. "It would certainly save you a struggle getting there with them and those boxes."

I really should have known better and would have done I'm sure, if my mind hadn't still been befuddled by being unable to find anyone to help me. After all, the carriage was going in the wrong direction in any case, and here was I, a complete stranger, stepping out from cover to....

"Bloody fool!"

I had a muddled glimpse of a dappled grey horse veering wildly to one side at my sudden appearance, and a woman; her face red splotched with anger, fighting to prevent the carriage from overturning.

There was a smothered gurgle of laughter and I took a moment's grace to cast a baleful glance in that direction, then hurried to where the carriage had come to an uneven halt, with one of its front wheels deep in the ditch. The horse, trembling uncontrollably, stood jerking its head up and down in agitation.

"Why involve me in your suicide? There's a flooded quarry no more than a mile along the lane. You might have considered drowning yourself in that instead!" Dismounted from the carriage, the woman had hurried to the horse, and was standing with its face between her hands, gentling the fright out of it.

"I-I'm sorry...!" She was undoubtedly classically beautiful when anger wasn't turning her face a colour to clash with the red of her hair. Her lips maybe just a shade too thin and her eyes perhaps a degree too cold, but I was aware that my sudden appearance in front of her carriage might well have been the cause of that. In any case, there was no disputing the narrow waist, or the full breasts filling her rich green dress to perfection.

"Sorry!" She echoed, cutting off my apology at source, and the message filtered through to my senses that this was perhaps not the moment to be eyeing her admiringly. "I should damn well think you are! What do you mean by jumping out in front of me like that and frightening the horse?"

"I-I'm sorry...." I began again with no greater success.

"So you said." The woman interrupted tersely.

"I was wondering, hoping, that you might be able to help me." I battled on gamely, determined to pursue my objective now I had committed myself so far. "I have to get to the pub where I've taken rooms you see, I thought that perhaps you might be kind enough to...."

"You have business in the village?" The woman interrupted brusquely, still not looking my way. Her horse, growing quieter by the moment, continued to receive the bulk of her attention. "Business of what nature"

"My name is Mark Montgomery, and I'm the new parish clerk here."

"Mark Montgomery you say?" Did I get a message from you about the lack of gravestones in the churchyard?"

"You probably did I sent a request for help to most people in the village. Most of you failed to reply though."

"Well we'll have to see if I at least can rectify that. I'll see you at the Hall tomorrow morning promptly at ten, to discuss this matter further. Good day."

Printed in Great Britain
by Amazon

53d97811-0ba8-40f3-bc75-f4d890e7ace4R01